Into the Dark

Jenny Leidecker

ISBN-13: 979-8-9868726-0-5

This book is dedicated to my mom,
Terry Routon,
for all the ghosts and demons she battled
for me first.

Also by Jenny Leidecker

Shhh
Invisible
Lucky
Caged
Solitary: A Short Story Collection

www.jennyleidecker.com

ONE

The Beginning

It's the first memory that slams itself to the forefront of my mind when I'm asked about my childhood. In all honesty, it's the first thing about my life I remember at all. It's not pretty, and even with years of therapy, I'm always thrown back into it. Although now, it's not a place of pain, only a snippet in time that I can't change or, for that matter, never had the ability to control in the first place.

That's probably where that need started. The need to be in control and have some semblance of structure and support. Over the years, I've managed to latch onto too many options that weren't good for me in that search, but now, now I think I've found it. Maybe, who the hell knows anymore. I'm just a line on a page at this point. I can see that I'm real, but do I exist as a fully formed character in this world? Some days I wonder myself, but back to that memory.

I know it's probably not entirely accurate, but the sticky parts, those are real, and I remember every second of those. We were living in a two-story old white house in a small town on the eastern side of the Pine Curtain here in Texas. I don't remember the yard, which is odd seeing that I was three and four at the time, you'd think I'd remember what it was like to walk out the back door, a small patch of grass, or even what the fence might have looked like, but I don't. When I think back on that house, I see it on the top of a hill with this long bright white, concrete driveway heading up beside it and disappearing behind it. Honestly, I'm not sure I've ever even seen a picture of that house to know if I'm right or not. Even the parts that I think I remember about the inside, they're likely just filler I've added around the swarm of chaos and emotions I felt during such a short amount of time.

Back to that memory, I was just three, standing up and crying in my crib. I can almost feel my feet as they bounce off the mattress, my toes curling into the blanket and sheet before launching me off the bed once more. I feel like the crib was white, but it's not important, I guess. I was a small child and contained within my own little safe space there. The walls throughout the whole house feel dark, stifling. I'm sure they were wood planks or maybe even wood panels. Again, I was just a baby, and it's such a small part of the story. My room felt massive, like it was just this empty space with only my crib and the wood painted a dingy baby blue on one wall. You'd think it would be pink, me being a girl and all, but it was probably just the nursery from whoever lived there before us. Maybe they had a boy, or perhaps I'm back to mental filler instead of actual memories.

I wasn't bouncing in my bed for joy though.

Remember, I'm crying in this one, and around me the screams were deafening. I'm not sure if I knew what was really happening or if I was just trying to cover up the sounds of her begging and crying? It was a big house, I know that much, so why this all had to culminate in my 'safe space,' I don't know. Maybe to show me what he was capable of or to show her how little she actually mattered in this world. I don't remember a single word spoken at that moment, but I remember the crying, the screaming, the begging, and the angry yelling filling the room and bouncing back off the walls, creating some kind of torturous echo.

I didn't know what was happening. That's not true, I was three. I didn't quite comprehend what it meant that she was standing there pregnant either. I knew there was a baby in her belly, but that equated to a doll for me, not a real life. Almost a figment of my imagination that didn't really exist. I couldn't see any baby, only a belly getting larger. Like they tend to do.

Toddlers have some understanding, sure, but how much, really? So that part of the equation, the baby, this imaginary being, didn't register for me, but it most assuredly did for her. Maybe that's what I remember her screaming back at him, to stop or he was going to hurt the baby. Hell, I'm positive that this wasn't the first incident like this during those eight months she had been pregnant. Come to think of it, I'd have to be naive to believe it hadn't happened during my own gestation. What a horrible thought to consider.

That's the one part I remember the most. The part that I can still see each and every movement, facial expression, and silent scream playing out as if it's on a never-ending choreographed loop. It's that moment she's sent flying across the room. There she is, my mother, eight months pregnant with what will soon be my sibling, being pushed and sent careening into the wall behind her. Not by some intruder there to rob us or anything you might expect it could be. Although I can see where that would be an option to consider. Those hands flinging her across the room belong to my father. The one person who vowed to love and cherish her was doing anything but. He apparently interpreted those words to mean hit and abuse until they cower in submission. I'm not sure where it all got mixed up for him during the education process, but he obviously missed a few things.

Strange, but I don't remember anything after that. It's as if the movie trailer suddenly ends, and you're left wondering if you could sit through an entire horror movie like that or not. Trust me, there were several moments I wished I could have walked out of the theater and asked for a refund. Unfortunately, the exit signs weren't lit up for me. At least not until my mother found the switch to turn them on way too many years later. But she did find us a way out, eventually.

It's turned into one of those odd moments at dinner parties or an uncomfortable turn of the conversation when the people around you start to talk about their first memories in life. It's always exciting for me to hear these cute and funny stories surrounded by love and warmth that their lives were catapulted from. Then there's always that dreaded moment. It happens every time. When that one person turns to me and says, "what about you, Jen, what's your first memory?" They never know this is the wall they're walking into headfirst. I've managed to deflect or change the subject a couple of times, but more often than not, I end up being the one who sucks all of the fun out of the room for a few minutes before someone finds a way to push past it. I keep a few light-hearted subject starters in my back pocket for when these moments arise, but it always looks like one of those, "so what did ya think about the game last night" type of comment, but hey, a save is a save.

To be honest, I'm fascinated with their happy memories, but I'm not jealous of them. My life hasn't always been filled with screaming and abuse, and I'm able to see how I grew from these moments now. I'm not going to lie, it took several years to get there, but I did. I'm getting ahead of myself, though. Let's keep going from here, shall we?

TWO

The House

It's funny how that house ends up in several of the stories from my childhood. I see flashes of what I think must be that house, but I'm honestly not sure if it is or isn't. I've heard memories recounted from my mom, my aunt, even a great aunt or uncle at one point, some I've even listened to from my father, but well it's always been difficult to listen to him speak without the rage film playing in the background occupying my thoughts.

Like I've said, I was practically a baby when we lived there, and so many thoughts and memories get jumbled together at that age. However, it's always been the one house growing up that stuck to my ribs, I guess you could say. Funny enough, it's the only one I ever dream about too. Forty years later, and its walls still haunt my dreams.

There are a few stories about that house, and I've heard at least on from anyone who ever walked through its door. It's always been 'that one haunted house we lived in' when people bring it up. Every last one of them has a story, even me. Now, I'm not concerned with whether you believe in the afterlife or not or even if you believe in ghosts or not. I've seen enough to believe for all of you. Just keep an open mind and take it for what it is, someone else's memory of events, and each one is valid.

My aunt came to stay there with us at one point, and she hated every second of it. Her story always starts with how there was a door at the bottom of the stairs, so you could close off the top floor of the house from the bottom one. I suspect it was to aid in heating and cooling purposes, but who knows. We've all been inside of those homes that have quirky little designs that you're really not sure what the thought process was when they were building it. This was probably just one of those. Anyway, my parents had gone out, and there was still no baby, but my aunt was there to watch over me. My room being upstairs, she left the door open in order to hear me in case I woke up crying or any of those other things toddlers do. She was only nineteen or twenty, I suppose at the time, and well, being the first niece, I was, of course, her favorite.

Like I said, just a typical night for a teenage babysitter. She was on the couch watching television when suddenly the door to the stairs shut. If I remember correctly, it was winter, for what that's worth in Texas, and she just assumed it was a draft that caught it and made it close. Not wanting to neglect her duties as my caregiver for the night, she got up and opened the door, and went back to whatever it was she was watching. She had just enough time to settle back into her seat when the door shut for the second time. Looking over her shoulder at it completely closed and aggravated that she was being pulled away from her show, she walked over and opened it again. This time, she realized that the heat wasn't on, and there was no draft there to close it like that with so much force. By the fourth time she had to get up to open the door, she was more than shaken and about to head up to get me from my bed or at least check in on me when my parents arrived home. She explained to them what had been happening, and well, it wasn't even at the top of the list of creepy things that had happened to them in that house.

Needless to say, my aunt refused to ever be there alone again. She wasn't the only one either by the time we were ready to move out of there. Too many strange things happened to everyone who crossed the threshold and was there long enough to pay attention to any of it.

Now I'm not sure, but I somehow recall stories of dishes being flipped upside down in the sink overnight and voices heard through the walls. I think I even had an uncle once say that we were all headed out of town, and an arm reached out of the attic door and waved goodbye. He never stepped inside it again after that either.

I don't know what to believe, but I'm sure there's some truth to it all. I've been back to that little town since, and the house is gone, and all that's left is a concrete slab. So, I can't even visit those ghosts to see if there's any validity to these stories or not. What I can tell you are the ones I remember.

So many of my memories start in that house, including all of the ones where, you guessed it, I lived with ghosts. I'm not sure that this is at all necessary in telling you my story, or maybe it is the story? It's definitely interesting, and well, who doesn't like an exciting ghost story? That's rhetorical; I'm going to tell them to you anyway.

I always see her when I dream of that house. It's the only time I can pull the memory of her so vividly. Lost in a dream of dark walls and pain. That house was filled with so much of that true pain, that seeped into the soul of it, but I've always known she wasn't the only one there. It was as if she kept me protected from the others that seemed trapped within that space with us. That is what we all were, trapped. My father trapped within his own pain and hate, using those as an outlet of some twisted definition of love, unable to break free from his own demons to see how he was only inviting more to the table and handing them out as gifts to those around him. My mother was trapped by fear and some obligation to try and make it work, to build a better life for her children, and with each new bruise creating some false representation of what she began to believe she deserved. My soon-to-be partner in crime, just waiting to be born, they were trapped in a completely different way. Trapped in silence, unable to even scream out their dissenting vote in the matter. They'd find themselves trapped in the same way I was soon enough. Caged within a house, you can't change, filled with hurt and hate that you can't escape, and making friends with the demons being gifted to you at every turn.

That is what she ended up being for me, a friend. Somehow, I knew she wouldn't hurt me, but again, she wasn't the only soul trapped there, and they weren't all as caring as she seemed to be. I guess I had my own little version of Mary Poppins. Of course, mine was dead, but she had looked over me while we lived there. I don't know when it began, memory filler starts to take over if I try to think about it too hard, but she'd appear to me every night, smiling. I'm sure that would creep out a lot of people, but I've always been the kid that knew the character of a person when meeting them, dead or alive, I guess. But if you're a genuine and kind person, I can sense that in you, even when others can't or choose not to because they can't get past how you look. Of course, if you're an asshole, I pick up on that too. You can hide from everyone else, but I always see you. I know who you are.

She always made me feel safe and loved during those visits late at night in my room. I'm sure so many of you are thinking, oh yeah, three-year-old and her imaginary friend, or something like that. Let me stop you right there, she was as real as you and I. Only, I mean, she was dead.

My mother thought that same thing for a while herself. I was just her silly little girl talking to my imaginary friend. Most children have them. I suppose it's an everyday occurrence for a lot of parents with small children. One of my kids even had a friend named Ernie, and no, not Bert and Ernie. Trust me, I asked. My mother didn't question my 'friend' until I began recounting stories I couldn't have possibly known. I'd present her with classic fables or stories at the breakfast table, ones that she barely knew or remembered herself. When I started singing songs she had never heard, she asked where I had learned them from. My answer was always the same that the lady in my room told me. You know, I'm sure she had a name, I'm sure she would have told it to me, but I've never been able to remember if she did.

Even in my dreams of her, she's just the lady in my room.

I was always happy when she was there. Like I said, she made me feel safe somehow. It was the moments after she was gone that threw me back into what was quickly becoming that well-known feeling of fear. She'd fade away at some point, and I'd be close to sleep, the edges of twilight when you can feel your dreams starting to pull at you. It wouldn't be long, and that warm feeling would fade, and everything would turn cold. I never remember seeing what it was or who it used to be or however I should be describing this thing, but I knew it was there. Not the loving feeling I had when the lady was with me, but hate, pain, and malice seemed to fill the room. Surrounded by all the things I tried to escape when I closed my eyes and no way of getting away from it either. I could feel them trying to suffocate me with every breath.

I'd lay there as long as I could, and sometimes it would leave, a reprieve from the fear, but most nights it stayed. I must have known I wasn't safe there, and I'd run out looking for some comfort from it all, some escape. My parent's room just down the hall, and they'd find me on the floor curled up outside their door every morning. I don't know why I was safer there or why it didn't follow me, but I spent several nights sleeping on the floor rather than my bed while we were in that house.

I'm not the only one who felt that spirit and knew just how real it was either. My father, the cruelest and strongest person I knew up to that point, was petrified of it. Looking back on it all now, I'm sure it must have felt like his own personal demons toying with him each time he raised a hand to my mother. Karma hovering around the edges waiting to clear his debt. Although, it didn't ever stop him from doing it again and again. It's one of the few stories he told that I actually remember. For some reason, I was able to focus on that one. Maybe it was because I knew exactly what he was talking about. I understood the fear he was trying to explain.

There was this one room in that house that no one ever wanted to be in, ever. My mother once said that it could be well over a hundred degrees outside, and that room would be damn near freezing. My father had been in an accident early on when we had first moved in, and he wasn't able to get up, and down the stairs, so they put a bed in that room for him to sleep in while he recovered. Before the first night was through, he had ripped the mattress off the bed and moved it into the living room. The man had been in the hospital for weeks and had practically been cut in half by a ton of steel that fell onto him, and he risked ripping every stitch from his abdomen and internally to get out of that room. I don't remember him telling me what he had experienced in there that first night, but he never went in there once the sun went down ever again.

He later turned it into the room he kept his motorcycle in so he could rebuild it, but he'd only work on it during the daylight hours and never with the door to the room closed. No one likes to be trapped inside with their demons, and he was no exception. The rest of the time, no one was allowed in there, not that any of them wanted to step foot inside of it anyway. Just thinking about the feeling of being within the proximity of whatever that was, gives me chills today. I can remember the coldness and hate that it radiated there, and no one was immune to experiencing it either.

That spirit still invades my dreams of that house too. It's almost as if it refuses to let go of me. Of course, those aren't really dreams. They turn into nightmares quickly for me. Well, not nightmares, not plural. It's the same exact nightmare each time. It's not a memory I have, not even a scene from some scary movie I've watched, but always the same. It's dark, and I'm walking through some suburban neighborhood, and I'm completely turned around. I can't figure out where I am, and I'm starting to panic at being lost. There's some van that pulls in at the end of the road, and it's waiting for me, stalking me. The panic increases and I turn to run back the way I've just come from, ducking between houses, hiding behind bushes, but no matter how hard I try to get away, I can feel that van and whatever is in it watching me. I've woken up several times from that nightmare over the years, only to fall right back into it again the minute I close my eyes. That spirit I once avoided in that house still haunts me, still stalks me. Only now, there's no running out of a cold room to curl up on the floor outside of my parent's bedroom. Now I have to find a way to face it head-on and force my way up to that van and to turn the tables. Turn it all from feeling as if I'm the hunted to making that fear my prey. Even old ghosts have the ability to be haunted sometimes.

THREE

The Deal

There's a switch that flips for all of us at a particular moment in our lives, isn't there? We start off life chasing ghosts, and it's fun trying to track down a dream that doesn't seem real or possible to anyone but ourselves. Then that switch, and you go from chasing ghosts to being chased by them at every turn. Every regret or lost opportunity haunting you. All of the different paths you could have taken, calling to you from some far-off place. The personal poltergeists clawing at our sanity and the purpose we've believed we are meant to serve within our lifetimes. The fear of having done it all wrong twisting at our insides and leaving us there a pile of 'what ifs' and wanting more. A feeling I'm all too intimate with, my switch flipped a while back, and it took me a minute to pick it all back up and reshape that pile into a real person, left held together by more ghosts.

It's a constant theme in my life, ghosts. One that most people shy away from or scoff at when it's brought up in conversation. There are always the believers, and then there are those skeptics that think how could you possibly hold stock in something so ridiculous. Most of those are the same kind of people who believe in some twisted ideology that essential oils can cure you of everything. Hard fact, there's no peppermint oil in a polio vaccine. Whether you believe it or not, doesn't really matter to me. Like I stated before, I've seen enough to believe for all of you, and be grateful you haven't.

That house, that first house I remember, that was only the beginning. My brother was born about a month after that first horrible memory of mine. He was a fat and perfectly happy baby, adding his voice into the screaming and chaos that already reverberated on an almost daily basis within those walls. I'm not going to lie; I tried to give him away to my mom's aunt there for a few hours as I sat in the waiting room of the hospital as my mother worked through labor. I was so set on having a sister, it was all I wanted. Not sure why it would matter to me, and if I try to overanalyze what could have possibly been running through a four-year-old's mind at the time, all I could potentially garner from it all is that boys were mean. Of course, my father wasn't the only male role model in my life at the time either. There were several of them, but he was that constant, that one man in my every day. Which meant boys were mean, and I wanted a sister.

So, out there in the waiting room with my brightly colored clay, fiddling about, I made a deal. If my mother showed up with a brother, my aunt could have him. However, if I had a new sister, she was mine. I suppose it's a good thing I didn't make this deal with the Goblin King, or it probably would have been added onto that list of regrets I mentioned earlier. My negotiation skills already at work at such a young age; I think I sealed the deal with a handshake, but only after I squirmed some candy and a soda from her first. Resolute in my decision, I was elated. I was going to get a sister, and if not, hey, M&M's were worth hanging out in a waiting room for a few hours. I call that a win any day.

I have no idea how long I was playing there after putting my potential sibling up on the auction block for any family member willing to bite (obviously, my aunt was a sucker to take that deal), before they rolled my mother out of the delivery room. There she was, swaddled critter in hand, and it was time for the truth. Was I going to be walking out of here with a new sister or just the faint chocolate memory already fading into oblivion? She rolled over this wrinkled bean in my direction and told me to say hello to my new little brother.

Dammit! This was not what I wanted at all, and my reaction was a family story that they still tell to this day. My great aunt looked down at me and announced to everyone else.

"Well, I guess he's going home with me?"

My response was immediate, and it rang true every day after that first meeting.

"No, he's mine. My baby. You can't have him."

My mother was, of course, slightly confused that her aunt was declaring ownership of this child she had just spent hours working hard to introduce into the world so he could experience those first moments of his life. That first moment that the air of this world enters our lungs and fills us with every possibility we could ever imagine. That's when it all begins, isn't it? I mean, we start off just this blob of wobbly skin and bones, but our futures are set into motion right there as the doctor pulls us free and slaps our asses. Happy childhoods are determined in that instant most of the time by those in the room surrounding you, those who will help shape you into the person you will become. Some of us are luckier than others. My brother didn't meet his utterly devoted caretaker until later, cloaked in the scented cloud of chocolate and clay and declaring ownership of his future understanding of love.

I became one of his lifelong ghosts. One that took care of him followed him, supported him, and even sometimes hurt him. Even today, as old as we are, after having searched out our own possibilities and creating our own lives and families, I am still one of those ghosts that haunts him, and he is one of mine.

FOUR

Lessons

I'm not sure how long we stayed in that house after my brother was born. I don't have a single memory of him and me there together. It's almost as if he didn't exist again until a year or two later. The screaming of this baby just blended into the screaming surrounding my life on a daily basis, making it hard to distinguish the two. Almost as difficult as it became to separate the differences between life and death. It's a concept most aren't familiar with until they're faced with the reality of it in some way or fashion. I, on the other hand, understood what it looked like, and the fear of death started early for me. Not my own; that's not a concept I accepted until much later in life. However, there are several times I know that I could have easily earned my ticket down the river Styx but somehow managed to avoid it.

The day after my brother was born, I came face to face with that fear. My mother had to stay another day in the hospital, and my great aunt had taken me up there to visit her. I was inconsolable, and turned into this wailing child in a waiting room proclaiming that her mother was dead. At the same time, my aunt did everything she could to try to convince a hospital full of nurses that I was not going to stop this tantrum without some concrete proof that my mother was, in fact, not dead.

For some reason, I was not allowed to go back to see her in her room. Who knows what the restrictions were at the time? But I was apparently too young to walk ten additional feet to see my mother lying in a bed recovering from childbirth. Maybe they were attempting to give her some short reprieve from the chaos she would soon face with two young children to care for. If they had only known that she was already a seasoned professional in the arena, or at least in theirs.

I'm not sure if it was my aunt's skills as a negotiator, which couldn't really be possible, I still got to keep my brother from the day before, or if it was the fact that children have developed the ability to create some of the most annoying and blood-curdling screams during the evolution process in order to get what they want, but the nurses found a way for me to be assured that my mother was not in fact dead. Instead, she was only being held hostage by some squeaky shod nurses who apparently hated child visitors in the maternity ward; this, of course, makes perfect sense somewhere in the crevices of my brain.

They rigged some sort of stool for me to stand on and look through the smallest pane of glass used in any building and rolled her just far enough out of her room that she could wave, and I could see her. That was it, their solution to the screaming banshee in the waiting area, a quick glance of my mother from the waist up. I guess when you're four, the simplest solutions are the best because I immediately stopped wailing, looked at my aunt, and told her I was ready to blow that popsicle stand and turned to leave. Bewildered at how easily that was remedied, I can only imagine the amount of side-eye she gave to each of those nurses in return. I wonder how many people had heard me declare my mother's death and the pain in my voice at what I was sure was an absolute fact at that moment. Did they pity me, or were they just annoyed by the tantrum of a toddler? Probably a bit of both.

I can't imagine why I would have thought my mother was dead that day. To my knowledge, no one had said anything of the sort, but then again, I've already established that some of these memories are faded and lacking in quite a bit of necessary detail. I think it was the fear of the loss. My mother hadn't come home, and there I was left with just my father. What was that going to look like? I can only conclude that I had come face to face with my biggest fear at the time, the disappearance of what I knew to be good, and an existence surrounded by all of what I knew to be bad. I was petrified. My world was flipped into a swirling ocean of fear for those few moments there in that waiting room, and all it took was a tiny pane of glass and a few short seconds to drag me back out of the riptide.

I have a few vivid, happy memories from that time in my life, but I'd be lying if I said I have many more than that. I remember this snoopy fishing pole I had, and lawn fishing with my great aunt and uncle in their yard with it. I was a seasoned fisherman, and you've never seen fish the likes of which I caught those days. Mainly because they were fake and served no other purpose than to make a toddler like me at the time squeal in delight. I still laugh as I picture it today. My uncle was on the other side of this hill in their yard, I couldn't see him from where I was standing, but he made sure my line was never reeled in empty. He'd attach that plastic fish onto my little plastic hook and tug on the line to let me know my bait was taken, and it was time to land my catch. Sometimes he'd make me fight for it, and I can still hear my own laughter, in those momenets, as I pulled between giggles and my aunt's encouragement. They showed me that success was not only possible but that it could be fun. Strange how that's the lesson I learned from a patch of grass and a few colorful plastic fish.

So many of those anecdotes that I carry with me started with the two of them. I'm glad I had those moments of fun and was allowed a short vacation from the realities of my life at home. My uncle taught me how to play poker when I was four, and by the time I was five, my nickel and dime container had more than his. I can still play the game well, but my poker face has all but disappeared over the years. I've since turned any gambling interests to roulette, a great opportunity to throw your hands in the air and give over control to something so insignificant as that tiny little ball bouncing around that wheel is. Everything else requires too much thinking to make it a gamble for me; just pick a number, and let's see what happens. Now that's a gamble.

There is one lesson that my uncle taught me that I hated learning more than any other, and it took a few times before it actually stuck with me, but once it did, there was no forgetting it. He had a unique way of punishing me, and to this day, I still try to imagine the things I missed in those moments I was made to ponder my decisions and actions. I was just a happy little munchkin, but I could find my way into some trouble without a doubt. Most of it included my mouth and its inability to figure out how to keep both lips touching for extended periods of time. My uncle never once swatted my butt or yelled down at me. He didn't even sit and attempt to find a way to intellectually reach my woefully underdeveloped mind either. No, he'd pull two kitchen chairs into the living room and set them right in front of the television.

One was facing the screen, and the other was facing away from it. I hated this punishment more than any other form I've ever experienced since, but it was utter genius on his part, and it taught me well. He'd flipped the channels to some cartoon and squeal in delight. I always hear Woody Woodpecker or Mighty Mouse when tossed back into this memory for some reason. I think it's because they were some of my favorites. There he'd sit to watch them all, and I'd have to sit and face away from the bright colors dancing across the screen. He'd laugh at what was happening and poke at me that he couldn't believe I was having to miss how that flying mouse was saving the day once more. I didn't have to go through this often, but it was torture when I did. There was a lesson there, though. It wasn't just some uncle of mine being mean and teasing a toddler while he watched cartoons, and I didn't. I learned that when you don't do what you need to do, you don't get to enjoy the things you want to do. I have failed in remembering it too many times since. To this day, the sound of Woody's cackle bouncing around in my head becomes a quick reminder, and I try to find my way back to being able to turn my chair around the right way and enjoy those moments in life I don't want to miss.

It wasn't all green grass and colorful plastic fish, and soon enough, I'd be back surrounded by the chaos of my life. Once we moved away from my aunt and uncle, things became even darker. Life became filled with muted colors with small patches of vibrancy here and there. Death and pain returned, and so did so much of the fear I had learned to live with, and that I had learned to accept as normal.

It was not normal.

FIVE

Severed

We must have moved about a year after my brother was born because I started school in one of those suburbs outside of Houston. Of course, the outskirts of Houston go on for miles. You're practically in Louisiana if you're living on the far east side of town these days. We lived close enough to the water that you could smell the salt in the air, but we were definitely not living it up on any beachfront property.

We had a trailer in some small beach community where all the yards seemed to be connected by gated chain-linked fences. You could cross in and out of your neighbor's yards on three sides of your property there. It was fun, like a maze of gates for all of us kids. I'd spend days working my way in and out of someone else's life for a time and then I'd be off to the next.

As it typically is in those close-knit communities, everyone knew everyone, and they all knew each other's business too. This was most certainly the case when it came to our family. It was a known fact that my father beat my mother regularly. It would have been difficult to hide the screams and the cries filtering out of our home as my father yelled anything and everything he could think of at my mother between raised hands. That god-awful green trailer housed a poorly kept secret, the likes of which everyone knew, and no one did anything about. I think that must be why all of our neighbors were so nice to me there. Surely, they felt sorry for the towheaded little girl next door. I know I would have, and a little part of me deep down still does.

This house, this is one, I remember way more things than I want to and even more I wish I could just forget. This, though, this is the place that started me out on my real journey; this is the one where I finally found myself. Is that even possible? Can a five-year-old find their purpose in life at such a young age? I tell you they can, or at least I did, but it wasn't the easiest thing to do, but I suppose it never is.

I hated and loved living there. I think it's because my world expanded while we were in that house. I walked with my mother every day to school and met people all along the way. It was the one thing my mother worried most about and the one thing she learned to let go of fairly quickly too. I knew everyone. I was that kid that never met a stranger in my life. The one that would walk up to anyone, no matter who they were or what they looked like and strike up a conversation. She recounts an instance when the discussion of me talking to anyone I meet arises. We had been in the park, you know the Mecca of our childhood, where swing-sets and teeter-totters are the altars for which our laughter and joy worship. There was a man sitting off to the side, not in a creepy sort of way, at least not as far as I was concerned. This wasn't just one of those parks for children, and I can only assume he had been contemplating his day as he strolled down one of the many walking trails available and stopped for a moment to catch his breath or attempt to soak in the laughter surrounding him as he sat himself down onto that bench.

My mother tells of how him sitting there alone had made her nervous. Many things often did in those days. In her defense, he was a large man and could have easily overpowered almost anyone in the park that day had he wanted to. I would imagine that sense of dread stuck with my mother for years after she left my father. She learned quickly that most men intimidated her and found that she'd pull out those examples of each bruise she locked away as a memory to cross-examine as a witness to the fact and justifying her fear. I, however, was unfazed by his size, and by his looming presence that must have felt to some like an overreaching shadow across the slides and jungle gyms. Before my mother had the ability to pull me back, I was on the bench climbing up right next to him. I think the word she's used to describing that moment was petrified. Not only was she scared that this man might snatch her daughter and run away with me, but she couldn't move, frozen in place. A prisoner of her own fear. We all have those reactions, don't we? Fight or flight are always the only ones you hear about, but more often than not, people respond by freezing, glued to that space their fear has cemented them to.

I can't remember his face, but I remember the moment. It's one of those times where purpose started to seep through into my life. Where knowing what I was doing was right, even if it might have looked wrong to others. He smiled down at me and didn't say a word, probably too scared to strike up a conversation with some random five-year-old girl in a park, but I saw him. Not just the man everyone else could see, this giant there to do who knew what to who, but him, and his sadness was radiating from him, and I could feel it.

I don't have a grasp of the exact words I used, but when I looked up at him, I just smiled and let him know that it was all going to be alright. I explained that he didn't need to be sad; she was happy and over there playing. He just kept staring, back to that freeze reaction, I suppose. I guess the effects of it had finally worn off my mother, and she was there nervously trying to shoo me away from him. I just sat smiling. As he shook off my comment, he looked even more confused in the direction of my mother. Again, I have no idea what was said, but according to her, they spoke for an hour as I slipped away to go play some more.

That man had lost his daughter just a few months earlier, and he would stop in at the park when he found the strength to do so and listen to the children laugh and play. The squeals of delight and all the kids running around without a care in the world allowed him some relief from his loss. He could sit and pretend for just a second that she might come around the corner of the slide and wrap her little arms around him once again. Death affects each of us differently. Some of us look for signs that our loved ones are free from pain or that they're happy, and some wallow in the memories, attempting to pull back some small part of them into the real world. Either way, they're never truly forgotten.

I don't remember that man's name, but each time he returned to the park, I'd go and curl up next to him for just a few minutes, smile up at him, give him a tight hug, and then I was off to the races again. He and my mother became friends of sorts, and after my welcome, she'd take my place on the bench beside him, and they'd talk while I played. He needed that. She needed it too. I like to think that her listening to this man's pain may have been the start of her working through her own.

Of course, there was still plenty of that to go around. Our home was still a war zone way too often, and I tried to keep to the outside of it as much as possible. The little boy next door and I were around the same age, and we managed many adventures together while we were there. You'd think I would have at least remembered his name. We were thick as thieves, the two of us. He was the first boy other than my baby brother that I saw with his pants down. The 'show me yours, and I'll show you mine' game was something I well remember. I didn't feel embarrassed about it. We all did it at some point, but I'm not sure I'd ever seen another human turn the shade of red he did. Wasn't even sure it was possible. He'd turn brighter than the strawberries we filched from the neighbor behind us when he was flustered. Seeing that was more entertaining than playing our game had been. He probably still blushes a little when he remembers it. I know I still giggle a bit at the memory.

Those strawberries, though, they count as another one of those vibrant memories while we lived there. The woman whose trailer was behind ours had the better part of her yard set up as a garden. I know she grew other things, but all I remember are those strawberries. All spring and summer, the 'show me' boy and I would sneak over there and grab one or two, shove them in our mouths, and run back into my yard, hoping no one saw us. She, of course, did every single time. We were worse than rabbits invading her garden, and after a week of watching the ill-equipped ninjas that we were, she gave in to our addiction.

If my mother couldn't find me wandering around our yard, you'd better believe she could look at the stoop of our neighbor's trailer, and there I'd be munching on strawberries like I'd never eaten a day in my life. I can still taste them if I think hard enough about it, fresh from the garden and warm. She'd toss them in a bowl with some cream and a spoonful of sugar; I've never tasted anything so wonderful in my life.

When I think back on that day, I'm positive that's where I was when she summoned me back into our upside-down kingdom. Have you ever seen those large wooden spools that electrical wire comes wrapped around? Not the kind you buy in the store, those that are used to run that all too important electricity from house to house that you see draped from pole to pole. My father must have done something along those lines at the time because I remember them everywhere, one in the yard, one as a coffee table, and one in the shed used as a worktable. I remember that one more than any of the others, though, and I can still close my eyes right now and see it.

Seeing it in my minds-eye is one thing. It's the sounds that are associated with that memory that I wish I could drown out and forget. One of the highlights of my childhood was my dog. Another one of those vibrant memories. That dog was smart and beautiful, and she watched over me everywhere I went. She's the reason my mother never minded me playing out in the yard alone or roaming around into different neighbor's yards all day. That dog protected me as if I were her own. I've never had another dog like her since, and I'm not sure I could find one that would make me feel as loved and secure as she did. As much of her own I might have been, though, this Doberman had just had puppies a few weeks before and she had some real momma work to do.

Did you know, the thing about Doberman puppies, is they're born with tails. Now, I've never seen an adult with one, although I'm sure they're out there. However, the lesson I learned that day was that they don't shrink or fall off as they grow older either. Had I not been exposed to enough trauma in my life, this one would have made it to the top of the list.

There they were, eight puppies wiggling around on this giant spool table, making those cute little puppy grunts, and nosing around for their mother. Innocent. Helpless. Just like me.

My mother had walked back into the house with my brother, and I was left there alone with my father and these puppies shut up in our shed. My dog was pawing at the other side of the door to get in, we had her babies, and she wanted them back. My father handed me a laundry basket with a towel laid out inside of it and gave me strict instructions to not let the momma dog inside just yet. I figured he was about to examine the puppies, maybe clean them, I didn't know. What I do know is that I wasn't prepared for what came next at all.

Grabbing one and holding it down against the

table, it began to cry out. I'm almost positive that had this puppy been able to choose between fight or flight, it would have handed over its boarding pass and ran onto the nearest plane to get away from my father, and I might have joined it. My dog on the other side of the door started getting more agitated at the sounds of her babies crying and clawed harder at the door. I stood in blissful unknowing for just a few seconds more. That is until my father lifted the cleaver that had been sitting on the table and swiftly brought it down, lobbing off this imprisoned puppy's tail.

I've never heard an animal scream before, but that's exactly what this wriggling ball of fur did, it screamed. The sound of that puppy bangs against a locked room in the corner of my brain where the things that sit and wait to haunt me hide. It never leaves, and every time I see a little puppy, the sound of that scream escapes that room for a split second, and I'm that little girl watching that cleaver come down once again.

I dropped the basket and began to wail that he had killed the puppy over and over. He lifted some goop out of a tub, smeared it where a once wagging tail had just been and snapped at me to pick up the basket and be quiet. He lowered what I expected to be the corpse of a puppy onto the towel, and it whimpered and nudged around again, looking for its mother. I'm not sure I took one breath between picking up that basket and watching that dog move, but I remember a feeling of relief to see that the puppy was, in fact, not dead.

The dog in the yard doing her best to claw her way into the shed didn't know that relief yet, and her bark was deafening. The scraping of her nails on the door turned desperate. I was trapped in a moment overwrought with the sounds of fear, pain, and desperation all around me. All of those emotions that seemed to ooze from people and apparently animals in my father's presence.

Seven more times, I watched as that cleaver was lifted and buried into the wood of that giant spool. Seven more times, I listened to the sound of a puppy scream out in fear and pain, and seven more times, I witnessed the goop added and another puppy wiggle its way into that towel. By the time it was over, all I could taste was the salt from my tears that were dripping from my face and down onto the towel below. My father looked at me as if I were some pathetic disappointment for not understanding the necessity of his actions, gathered up the tails, tossed them in the trash, and walked out the door. There I was left, another part of my innocence severed but still helpless.

SIX

Bobby

It couldn't have been too long after that when the police showed up. For once, they weren't knocking on our front door, which was surprising and confusing. Everyone else in our little community was amazing and not at all in need of the police showing up to tell them to behave better. So, what could they possibly be doing here for any of them?

It had to have been the summer. I remember the sun shining and glaring off the windows of our neighbor's trailer. My mother had pushed me back into the house so she could go and investigate what the need for the police might have been. Curious by nature, I snuck out the back and found my way through the maze of gates to the neighbor's house they had pulled into. I could overhear the officer talking to my mom and a few of the other neighbors, using words I didn't understand, except one. Dead.

I thought that was an odd thing to say, they had parked in the driveway of a neighbor that couldn't have been older than my mother at the time, and dead didn't make sense. At least not as much sense as it would have made had they shown up at the neighbor behind us. He was older than the world, and I wasn't sure he hadn't had a part in making it too. But they weren't at his door. Instead, they were at the quiet man's house just on the other side of ours. A few other people in loud cars had shown up by this point, and they kept walking in and out of his trailer, leaving the door wide open. Don't they know you're not supposed to let the air conditioning out? I had to see what was going on, maybe it was some kind of party over there. So, as stealthy as I had been sneaking into the strawberry patch before, I managed my way up to the steps to look inside.

It seemed dark somehow, only the sun reaching in through the windows and door illuminating small patches of the walls. I could see the dust particles floating around everywhere. They always look so beautiful to me, dancing in the air, the glitter of filth, I suppose. My nose barely reached the top of the stoop; I could see what looked like a big pile of blankets on the floor and what appeared to be a remake of some of my splatter paintings in red on the back wall. The puzzle didn't fit together for me right then, but I soon understood what had happened.

Ducking under the trailer as the men in their uniforms fumbled through the door with what looked like a bed on wheels, I crouched there listening to the inane chatter and laughter of their conversation. I have no idea what they were talking about. I barely remember the neighbor's name. I'm pretty sure it was Robert or Bobby or something like that, but I honestly don't know. What I do remember is watching them struggle with that rolling bed back down the stairs and across the gravel driveway to their vehicle. It looked like they had just picked up that pile of blankets and decided to give them a ride out of the house in style. I wondered what it would be like to sit on that bed and roll down the street. I imagined it would feel a lot like flying for a minute, and I almost jumped out to ask for a push.

They must have been about halfway across the yard before I realized there were shoes in that pile of blankets-Bobby's shoes. I'm sure it makes me seem slow or something, but I was only five, remember. They were just about to the ambulance before it clicked that those shoes were still attached to Bobby's feet, and that wasn't just a pile of loose blankets they were rolling down the driveway. That was Bobby. Sliding back out from under the trailer, I peeked inside once more, and the light shining through suddenly magnified the splatter on the wall. That red was a shade I knew all too well, having watched the blood drip from my mother's nose enough. The word 'dead' now made sense. Bobby was dead, and he'd left a great deal of himself dripping down his living room wall.

I looked over at the gaggle of adults, my mother included, wrapping up their conversation with the officer and quickly weaved my way in and out of the neighbor's fences and back in through my backdoor. I sat, trying to decipher what it was I had just seen. I had no horror movie reference, other than that of the real one I was living in, and well, there had been blood, but not that much blood. I knew that Bobby was dead, that much was certain. I just didn't know why he was dead or if what had happened to him was something that could happen to me. Could I explode in the living room and leave a mess like that? It wasn't a question I could ask my mother, or my ass would be glowing from the whipping I'd receive for sneaking over there in the first place. Thus began the beginning of one of my biggest fears in life, the unknown. I think that's why that van in my nightmare is so scary. I still don't know what's waiting for me there. I only know that it is.

Soon, the unknown and I would become close friends, and it all started on that summer morning peering in through that trailer door at the pieces Bobby had left behind.

SEVEN

The Closet

My father popped in and out of our lives during this time. He wasn't always there, and well, he wasn't always gone either. He'd leave under the pretense that he was off to work for a few days, and on occasion, it took him four or more days to run to the store for a pack of cigarettes and manage to find his way back home.

My mother must have felt like she was on a vacation from the worst parts of her life during those times. They were always there waiting in the corners, hiding, and looking for that perfect moment to jump out and remind her of her place, according to my father. There were many reminders.

It couldn't have been long after the Bobby incident that it was again time for one of those reminders. It had become a routine in our house. He'd be gone for a few days, come back, and everything would be tense, my mother questioning where he had been, and the lessons would begin. I was only five, and my little brother was one, old enough to walk, well, wobble anyway. So, it was easier to play with him now that he had some mobility. It was also easier to protect him. He was mine, after all.

The sound of raised voices was always the first sign, the one where I'd start to plan my escape. I couldn't actually leave the house, but I could grab my brother and find the escape hatch to one of our bedrooms. I'd pull the mattress partway off the bed, and we'd play in the makeshift fort with some of his toys, or when it was really bad, I'd shut us into my bedroom closet, and I'd tell him stories or read him books. Some of them were quite animated to drown out the screams reverberating off the trailer walls.

There was no doubt that this particular lesson was going to fall onto the 'really bad' list. The sounds of my mother slamming into the wall for the third time ensured that this was going to be an afternoon locked in my closet. I'm not sure what story I was making up for my brother that day, or anything about it for that matter, but I remember how easy it was to entertain him at that age. He'd sit there with me and laugh at the funny voices, elaborate gestures, and the occasional tickle for emphasis. I loved watching him laugh, and had it not been for the sounds of screaming and violence on the other side of the wall, it would be a perfect memory.

I'm not sure how long we had been sequestered inside of my closet, but at some point, my brother had given up on my form of entertainment and curled up on a blanket and fell asleep to discover his dreams instead. He can still sleep through anything, but I was always amazed how the sounds of them fighting didn't faze him as they did me. Being born into the chaos must have allowed him to find a way to press some internal mute button that I have yet to find within myself, but I'm still looking.

He hadn't been asleep long, and the arguing was nowhere near settling down. Trying to decide if I were going in search of my own visit to dreamland or sit and hope it all ended sooner than estimated by my previous experiences, when something caught my attention out of the corner of my eye. For a moment, I was petrified, I'm not afraid of many things, but I'd run into the fires of hell if that movement were the result of sharing space with a mouse. I may have been a diehard fan of Mighty Mouse, but a real honest to goodness furry long-tailed rodent, we were never going to be buddies.

To my surprise, sitting there in the far corner with his arms wrapped around his knees and pulling them tight to his chest was Bobby. You'd think that would have sent me running, but well, things like that never did. He wasn't the first dead person I'd seen, and I was slowly coming to the realization that he wouldn't be the last either. Looking back on it all, it might have been better that he had been a mouse instead. Just a blip on the radar of life, and a quick run through the house screaming and it would have been done. Honestly, I'm not sure anyone would have noticed my screaming and flailing like a crazy person if I had been running away from such a ferocious creature with four tiny little legs. Instead, it was just a continuation of what had started for me at the age of three and having a dead woman as a nightly caretaker for almost two years. It somewhat lessens the fear of other visitors that aren't breathing and taking up space like I currently was.

I don't recall a lot of our conversation there in the closet, but I do remember asking him the first question, "Are you ok?"

I don't know why, but it felt like one that no one had asked him in too long and one he needed to answer. He shook his head no and spent the next, I don't know how long, recounting what I think were all the things in his life that had gone wrong. He knew I was just a kid, and I can't imagine his spirit expected a then five-year-old to remember the struggles of a grown man's life. He had obviously found himself at a crossroads and consumed by sadness. That's what I remember, how sad he looked there curled up in my bedroom closet, knees to his chest as he released an army of demons he had lost the battle with about a week or so ago.

I'm not sure which one disappeared first, the sounds of my mother slamming into the hallway walls or Bobby, but they both managed to vanish as quickly as they appeared. Of course, I knew for sure that one of them would be haunting me again soon, and I figured it wouldn't be Bobby. As a matter of fact, I never saw him again after that chat in my closet, and I can only hope that he found some peace there sharing his story with me. I sometimes feel my own sadness when I can't remember any of the things he told me that day, almost as if a piece of him could have remained alive with that memory. I guess, in a way, he did. Memorialized in the past of a little girl crouched in a closet with her little brother sleeping beside her. A moment never forgotten, and neither is he.

EIGHT

Dreams

I'm sure it's strange that I can't remember a word from a twenty-minute conversation I had with some dead guy in my closet, but I do remember the dream I had that night. Dream is not the right word, nightmare. It wasn't the one with the van either, this one was different, but somehow, I knew they were connected.

My father's mother, my grandmother lived in an old antebellum-style home in the Piney Woods area of Texas, and it always felt like the biggest house I could ever imagine. It was old and beautiful, with a dark black mahogany staircase right inside the front entryway. I spent many summer days playing in that house, running up and down those stairs until someone grew tired of the sound of our footsteps and giggles as my cousins and I used those stairs as our own personal step machine. We'd be tossed into the backyard or onto the front porch, and we'd find another adventure at the decibel level the adults could handle.

There was a landing halfway up those stairs, and often we'd sit in that square and draw or play with our dolls. It was those stairs that dominated my dream that night. They had always been a fun place to play, a happy memory. That is until I had that nightmare. I was standing at the top of the stairs, looking over the railing into the foyer, the sun reaching across the floor from the stained-glass window of the front door. A rainbow of colors dancing up the first couple of steps, and I was giggling as I watched them. That carefree feeling and enjoyment of this place I knew well ended suddenly. The landing I had spent many days sitting and coloring on disappeared, and what was left was only a darkness. I'm not sure how else to explain it. It was nothingness. The light and airy feeling of the kaleidoscope of colors strewn across the floor disappeared, and the blackness, the emptiness began to spread like a rash up the walls and consumed the stairs one at a time.

I was left trapped at the top, nowhere to go for safety, all of the rooms behind me locked, leaving me there on those stairs waiting to be swallowed up by whatever this was. I could feel it as if it was alive. I could feel the anger and the hate swirling around in the darkness it created. It was the same as that ever-present evil being that haunted my days in that old house, the one that the lady in my room tried to keep me safe from back then. Only this time she wasn't here in my dream to keep whatever this was away. I was the only one there to fight against it, and I had no idea how. It had created a black hole filled with an unknowing there trapping me, and there was no escape to be found.

As scared as I was, there wasn't any panic. I don't know how I knew I could get away or that it wasn't completely real, but at one point, I could feel that I was only there to observe its power and not to be overwhelmed by it, at least not yet. I didn't wake up until all that remained was me holding tight to the newel post at the top of the stairs, surrounded by the darkness. It wouldn't be the last time that nightmare took over, and just as the van would continue to chase me all night, so would the darkness follow me up those stairs again and again. I couldn't escape it once it started, and each time I'd fall back asleep, it would be there haunting me once more.

I can recall how uneasy I felt that first time I visited my grandmother once these dreams began. It had to be closer to my sixth birthday; I remember a cake and blowing out my candles while we were there. As each year passed, my ability to ignore the things I could see around me grew thinner. I found that I could easily tell what people were feeling when I was in their presence, or if I touched certain people, how I was able to see flashes of them, almost like a movie. It didn't happen all the time, and it didn't happen with every person, but when it did, there was always a reason. I learned quickly that I somehow needed to deliver a message or let them know that I could see them for who they were in that moment. I imagine I came off as a weird little girl to so many people, but there was no stopping it.

I once had a teacher that touched my shoulder for a brief moment in line as we headed into the lunchroom when I was in kindergarten. It was an innocent enough gesture, just leading me along as they do, but as her fingers brushed against me, I was taxed with another task other than picking up a tray full of food and talking to my friends. I stepped out of line and tugged at her skirt, and when she acknowledged me, I told her what I knew.

"You're going to have a baby."

Now, this was not a woman who by any stretch of the imagination looked like she was pregnant, nor had she made any statement to this fact. When she looked down at me, you would have thought that I had just run over her dog, and her tears balanced on the edges of her eyes as she tried desperately to hold them back. Leaning down to look me in the eye, she simply let me know.

"Oh, Sweetie, thank you, but I can't have babies."

She was wrong. A month later, she found out she was pregnant, and that summer, she did, in fact, have a baby. I remember watching her belly grow all year, and whenever she was within arm's length of me, she would find a way to touch me. She'd squeeze my shoulder or hug me in line; she became one of my favorite teachers growing up. I don't know how I knew to tell her that or how I knew it would be true. I only knew that they were the words I had to speak to her before I could enjoy my lunch that day. She wasn't the first, and she would not be the last.

NINE

The Escape

This gift or curse or whatever it was, it didn't happen all the time, and I didn't see ghosts at every turn either. That was a real blessing. Could you imagine?

I had no control over what I knew about someone or saw around them each day, and sometimes it would be so long between incidents, I'd start to believe I had just imagined it all. I was a kid, after all, and we all know how active our imaginations can be at those ages. To be honest, I never lacked imagination, but I could never just picture things in my head either. I'm always amazed when people tell me that they can close their eyes and see themselves sitting on the beach or watch the water lapping at the shore. I can't do that. When I close my eyes, all I ever see is darkness. For a long time, I thought it was just the darkness in my dreams keeping me from seeing any of the light and fun I could imagine, but I'm not so sure about that.

Recently they came up with a name for it, and

I'm not the only one who can't picture things in their mind's eye. They call it aphantasia, and they say that people with this are unable to register a visual connection and that we are somehow stunted in some way. I may not be able to close my eyes and picture it, but I can calm my mind and feel it. Every emotion, every touch, and every sound echoing within that memory, I can call all of that back up as if it were happening right then. Just like when you hear a particular song, and it throws you back into another time. I've been known to taste the drink I was sipping on at the bar during a few Green Day songs or God help me, I still smile when I hear the remake of Cotton-eyed Joe because I instantly feel my best friend in high school dragging me across the dance floor, my heels sliding out from underneath me and almost busting my ass too many times to believe I was anywhere near sober while we were out at one of our weekend haunts.

My point is that maybe those of us who can't see the images in our minds are more susceptible to the physical and emotional memories. Perhaps we are the ones who are capable of drawing out those deep feelings from the people around us. Maybe we are the ones who have the gift of seeing ghosts or knowing when they're around. I've tried to explain that feeling to people before, and it's as foreign to them as their ability to visualize mental images is to me. I don't know how I know they are there, and I may not necessarily see them, but I always know when there's a spirit close.

I know there are a few of you shaking your head now, thinking this woman has lost it, and here we go off on another ghost story. I don't blame you. I've read enough of my own to probably walk into the same conclusion, but let's leave the ghosts for another moment. Soon.

I felt the shift in the air that day, something was off, and I knew things were different somehow. My father had just returned that morning from another trip to pick the tobacco himself since that was the only reason I could see why it might take him three days to go off and buy a pack of smokes. My mother didn't question him though, she didn't argue or accuse him of a multitude of nefarious activities. She was eerily calm and quiet. It was almost more unsettling than the swinging of fists and screams of 'stop' I had grown accustomed to. Following my mother's lead, I kept my head down and tried to keep my little brother as occupied as possible so as not to create any potential frustrations that were unnecessary.

We all went about our day as if he had never returned, other than my mother's required serving him his meals or whatever else he may have asked for. When it was time for bed, my father announced that he was going to walk a few houses down to a friend's and have a few beers. He'd be back drunk in a few hours, and I would expect to be woken by the sounds of their arguing before the sun rose tomorrow morning. This was not going to be a fun night for anyone. That wasn't a prediction pulled out of thin air; that was a guarantee from experience.

My mother watched him walk down the street for a few minutes until he turned into our neighbor's drive, and he stepped inside. He'd be gone for hours, and I was hoping to sleep for those few quiet moments while I could because the war would be starting earlier than I wanted any alarm to wake me. She turned and sat my brother and me down on the couch, flipped on the television, and told me to keep him occupied.

She hurried up and down the hallway a few times and rushed in and out of her room and ours. I'd see her carrying something here and there, but I never could tell exactly what it was she was doing. I figured she was putting up laundry and cleaning before he returned home and used it as an excuse to start a fight with her.

It couldn't have been, but ten minutes later she came down the hall with a suitcase and a big black trash bag full of something. She slipped out the front door, and I could hear the car doors open, and the sound of the makeshift luggage bounce across the seat. She nearly flew back into the house, grabbed her purse, the keys, and my brother, and like ninjas, we slipped into the darkness and into our car. She told me to sit on the floor until she said different, and my heart started in at a hundred beats a second once she turned the key. I thought for sure he would hear it, that he'd come running out of the other trailer and pull her from the driver's seat and beat her right there in front of everyone. He didn't.

I don't know how far down the road we were before she told me to get up in the seat and put my seatbelt on, but I didn't recognize where we were, and there wasn't a trailer in sight. We didn't stop until we pulled into the driveway of my grandparent's home just across the river. Far enough away, he couldn't walk there, but not far enough away, he couldn't show up at the front door tomorrow. As my mother unloaded us out of the car and grabbed the suitcase and trash bag out of the backseat, she looked down at me and only said one thing, and for a second, I believed her.

"We're safe now."

We were, for the night, but tomorrow was another day, and no one knew what the sun would bring.

My grandparents must have been expecting us or at least hoping we were going to escape because they were waiting for us at the back door, hugs, and kisses at the ready. I remember this house, but I've been told over the years that I have it all wrong. I'm not sure if I believe them or if I just don't care who's right. I can see it laid out the way I remember it, and I've pictured it too many times to be too off base with it all. The truth is, I'm almost positive that I've combined the layout of two different houses into one, and all the memories of my time spent within them exist in this hybrid home.

That night, the three of us cuddled together in one of the spare bedrooms. The bed was large enough for us to sleep comfortably, and I tried to pretend like I wasn't scared, but I was more scared than I had ever been. What would happen if he came here? Would he hurt my grandparents too, or would he grab my brother and me and take us away from my mom and run away forever? That was the worst thought, being forced to stay with him, to be left with that unknowing of what could possibly happen. My biggest fear always being, what I can't see or what I don't know. I hate guessing, and this night was full of a six-year-old girl trying to guess what could or would happen next. We had gotten away for tonight, but that was only hours, there were still days ahead of us where anything was possible.

At some point, my tired little body won over

the hamster spinning on its wheel in my mind and put him in his cage for a while. I don't remember dreaming that night, which is probably for the best, but I could feel my mother alternate between tense and finally relaxed. It was as if a switch kept flipping within her, and when she'd tense, I'd feel it so deeply it would drag me out of sleep and into her fear. There are moments when the way others feel can drown you. There I was in that bed, and I was struggling to tread water.

I'm not sure when the sun started filtering through the window, but when I opened my eyes, I was there in that bed alone, and I panicked. It had happened, I knew he had come and taken them, and I was left alone, on my own. When the voices and the sound of my brother's laughing bounced down the hallway, I nearly cried. I can still feel the air rush into my lungs as I gulped at it, realizing I had been holding my breath since I woke up frozen in fear.

I couldn't believe we were all suddenly alright with a mere change in location. If that had been the case, each time he'd left should have felt like an escape in itself, but we always knew he'd be back. I knew that morning that he'd be back, and there would be no stopping his wrath brought on by us leaving. It's like living perpetually in that moment when you're on a roller coaster, you've been climbing higher and higher, and you've just reached the top. There's that second when you can feel the front cars pulling at the back and ready to make that dive, but you're held there, teetering between climbing and falling; that's where I existed that morning, between the struggle with my fear and the release of it.

Everyone else went about the morning as if there wasn't this looming unknown just outside the front door. I couldn't pretend that it didn't exist, and I wasn't willing to believe it was all over, and that the chaos I had been born into suddenly ceased to be. The darkness was consuming the walls around me and swallowing up everything in its wake, and that van was parked down the road, watching and waiting for me to turn in fear, and this time, I couldn't wake up.

TEN

Family

I enjoyed spending time with my grandparents. Their house was always so full of so much love and laughter. My grandfather was the type of man who loved to joke around, and his use of quick wit and sarcasm were passed along to me in spades. My grandmother wasn't the type to stand for it all and didn't find him nearly as funny as he found himself. She was a strong woman that didn't allow him to get away with his poking fun in her direction very often. Those instances he could make her laugh, make her crack a smile, those were the moments he lived for, that he fought to win. There were always laughs, though. Along with so many inside family jokes that it's hard to recall even a sliver of them now. Each person who grew up in their presence has their own list of those they cherish and remember. No one was exempt from my grandfather's jokes or his teasing. The one thing I always remember people saying, if he wasn't making fun of you, he didn't like you. I had seen examples of that fact many times. If nothing else, he was consistent when it came to how he treated everyone.

Everyone was family if you walked through their door, and it took a lot to be disowned in their eyes. This whole situation was going to test that theory. My father was obviously family, but did he deserve to be considered that any longer? Did any of us deserve to be subjected to that kind of family anymore? God, I hoped not.

My uncle walked in while I sat at the kitchen table shoveling some sugary cereal into my mouth. I hadn't heard him open the front door, and his sudden appearance scared me enough that the hand holding onto my spoon jerked and flung cereal across the table. It was written on his face how easily he could see the ball of fear so tightly wound within me, and a shadow of sadness crossed over him before he had an opportunity to hide it. He tried to play it off, but when you're a kid like me, you see every nuance there is, if you miss one, you might not make it to the closet to hide fast enough.

He was a towering man, and when you're that little, a man well over six feet felt more like he could have easily been ten or fifteen feet tall instead. A giant in my world, but a gentle one, as I've found, comes with the territory in men that size. It must be something in the air up there that the rest of them just don't have access to. My brother walked over and grabbed him by the hand in hopeful anticipation, and my uncle followed through in granting that wish. Lifting my brother off the ground, dangling from his hand, he couldn't control the giggling pouring from his little body. Shouts of "higher, higher," pushing past the smiles when he could get them out. I couldn't help but join in his excitement and start laughing myself. My brother smiles with his whole face, it practically wraps around his entire head when he's that happy, and I was always saved from my fear and sadness by the sounds of his happiness.

Around the hundredth time my uncle lifted him in the air, I think his arm was ready to give up. Putting him down for the final time, the toddler tantrum started but didn't get that far. If my uncle looked ten feet tall to me, he must have looked like the giant Jack ran from after climbing up the beanstalk to my brother. Realizing he couldn't argue and win with a giant, he turned tail and ran in search of someone closer to the ground that he could sucker into doing his bidding next.

Walking over and tousling my hair, he smiled again. This time there was only a hint of the pity and sadness he felt for me. I know how difficult it is as an adult to see children struggle with issues they should never have been exposed to. I've looked at other children the same way my family looked at my brother and me after they knew the truth of what my father was and the things he did to my mother. He couldn't help but express those feelings, couldn't keep from thinking that I'd never get to be just a normal little girl in a normal world. As if normal really exists anywhere anyway.

I'm not sure when my aunt arrived, but true to my family, this was a moment for circling the wagons. By the end of the day, every member, whether by blood or by invitation, was there to support my mother and to do whatever they could to help us in our escape from the whirlwind of life we had been enduring for so many years. There were a few times that day that I think my little body relaxed and just played. All of my cousins arrived, and we ran around the backyard screaming and laughing like banshees filled with joy. That's the way children are supposed to feel, safe and full of joy; free to be who they are in those few precious years of life where the only care they truly have is how still can I stand during freeze tag?

That's how my day ended, but as expected, the chaos found us. I knew we hadn't really escaped that night, and I knew he was going to find us eventually. It wasn't as if my mother had all too many places to go, and it doesn't take a smart man to realize that his battered wife likely ran to her mom and dad for the comfort she needed. My aunt and uncle were the only other family there when the tornado that was my father blew through the house. I know now that this possibility was the reason my uncle arrived so early that morning, our family bouncer of sorts, I guess. This would easily become a day that memory couldn't forget. One I'm sure will join in the others imprinted on my brain that will flash before my eyes when it's my turn to leave this world. I can almost close my eyes and imagine them all if I wanted to, but I definitely don't want to, and I'll keep that film on the shelf until it's time for its final showing.

I was at the kitchen table again, the heart of every home I remember being in growing up. Colors were strewn in front of me, and some coloring book full of empty pages just waiting to be filled by the aspiring artist I felt I surely would become at that time. My little hands carefully trying to stay within the lines of what was undoubtedly a masterpiece in the making. It was sudden, like that first crack of lightning. You're never quite sure if you really saw it, and you look around waiting for the thunder to break through the clouds for confirmation that the storm is close. That storm, my father, blew through my grandparent's front door in a cloud of fury and determination. I could hear the thunder that was his voice reverberating off the walls, and I sat frozen in mid brushstroke of the happiness I had been trying to enjoy.

Through the kitchen doorway, I could see my mother backing away from him quickly, stopped only by the wall in her way, or she would have kept scurrying backward for eternity. There were only a few times I actually witnessed my father strike her, but the sound was unmistakable and one I knew all too well for a young girl of six. His hand came down hard against her face, as his other hand reached for her throat but never meeting with its intended target. My uncle appeared out of nowhere, and I'm not sure where he had been when all of this started, but he was there now, almost as if he had appeared out of thin air, and I think for a second, I could hear Mighty Mouse declaring, "Here I come to save the day!"

Without a word, my uncle wrapped his arm around my father's neck and pulled him through the house on his heels. I watched, frozen in my chair, color still in hand as he flailed past me, and for the first time, I saw that all too noticeable look of fear in his eyes. My grandfather padding behind with more anger in his step than I had ever witnessed in him before. My full of laughter Papa was suddenly the dad he had been to his daughter well before I had an opportunity to meet him, and it was clear that you didn't hurt his little girl. A lesson I believe my father learned the hard way that afternoon.

I'm not sure exactly what they did to him out there, but I can imagine it was an attempt to return every ounce of pain he had inflicted on my mother over the last several years. As scared as I had been in those moments watching my mom back away, I found relief in seeing my father pulled through that door. Somehow my mother's words from the night before felt more real after that and turning back to the book in front of me, I could breathe. We were safe now. There would be many more, but this storm was finally over.

ELEVEN

Grandma

We lived with my grandparents for a few years after our escape, and to go from a house filled with screaming and pain to a house full of joy and laughter changes your life rather quickly. I'm not going to deny that my childhood wasn't traumatic, it was, but the trauma team that is my family saved us and brought us all through the healing process. We were never a burden to any of them, and all we ever felt was love from that day forward. The only time I was hiding in the closet was because it was the best place to not be found when I wasn't 'it' during our marathon hide and go seek games. All those memories faded into the background, stowed away in some back room of my mind where the file clerk only wandered in for reference when prompted to fetch something here and there.

My grandmother was an interesting woman. You didn't cross her, but you were never rejected by her either. I can say that her influence on my life helped to mold the strong and independent woman that I grew into. She didn't say a whole lot, so when she spoke, you listened, and there were several times I crossed paths with her that sent me outside in search of my own switch from the wisteria in the backyard. You ever had to do that, pick your own switch? That is one of the most nerve-wracking errands I had ever been sent on in my life. Too thin, that sucker would sting like fire, but too thick, and she'd go pick her own, and God knows I only picked wrong once. Of course, that's also how I learned that those real thin ones would make you want to find a way to melt into the furniture in an attempt to get away from it too.

Now, I didn't get the switch every time I found myself in trouble. I'd likely still be unable to sit down today had that been the case, but I felt its sting more than I care to admit too. She wasn't all discipline either, and throughout my whole life, she was the one person I knew I could always confide in without any judgment waiting for me on the other side. There's a reason for that, one that many people noticed but never had any real understanding of. That's not their fault. It just didn't make sense to them at all. But it made sense to me, and it wasn't long after we moved in with my grandparents that I realized why her words were important. I learned that my ability to know things, to feel things wasn't just me in our family, but it also wasn't something anyone talked about.

It's one of those subjects that people either want to dive right into or where they look at you like you escaped an institution recently, and they start looking around for the men carrying nets. I've been on the receiving end of both of those scenarios, and neither is necessarily my favorite. Some play it off as intuition, where others talk to you as if you've made it all up for attention or that Casper must have surely been your favorite cartoon growing up. I can say that there are many days that I'd wish any of those possibilities had been true, even the institution. Seventy-two hours in a room to myself, could have been a welcome relief a few times. There are days, though, where I'm glad I've been a witness to the things I've seen and to the people I've touched. That's something you can't replace. The look on the face of someone who's been given just the right message at just the right time, a sense of joy and understanding comes over them. That makes it worth it.

My grandmother was the head of the family, in a way. She had a chair in the den, it was her chair, and no one else dared to sit in it, other than the random grandchild that managed to waddle over and climb into her place. It was at the head of the room, almost as if she were set up as royalty there in that plush brown floral monstrosity. If she wasn't at the kitchen table, you could always find her in that chair. She'd sit there and stare off as if she were watching the television or looking down at some puzzle or needlepoint, but if you watched her eyes closely, she'd follow things that weren't there. Things that other people either couldn't or chose not to see. That is until we moved in there. It's important to know that you couldn't lie to my grandmother. She could pick it out as a lie before you were finished with your first sentence. You always knew she could see right through you too, and she'd just look at you, waiting until you were prepared to start over with the truth instead. A human lie detector of sorts, and this was one of those mornings she looked over at me and sat in wait for the truth to spill out.

I'm not sure if it was the movement around us I noticed first or the movement of her eyes as she skimmed the room. I had known she was there. I'd seen this teenage girl walk through the den dozens of times over the month or so since we made this our home. She was always around, but she hadn't noticed me noticing her, I guess, or she just didn't want to be bothered with some little girl, I'm not sure. I guess it was about the third time I had followed her steps through the den and, well, through the back door, that I could feel my grandmother's stare boring into me. Her eyes felt like lasers pointing right at me, anticipating my next move, waiting to see what story I was going to spill out to her. I could tell by the way she was looking at me that she knew, and the existence of that wisteria and the possibility of a switch was a real threat at that moment. I wasn't about to press my luck and lie, not to her, and I didn't.

TWELVE

Did you see that?

"Did you see that?"

It seemed like the safest question and the best way to answer that look she was giving me. I knew she had. I knew from that first day I sat and watched her in that chair pretending to be preoccupied that I wasn't alone. My mother never saw them. She never picked up on the movement of someone there that wasn't physically manifested existing around her. That's not to say that she didn't sense them on occasion, she most assuredly did, but she never followed the faint impression of the dead moving through the world in her presence. Not like I did, not like my grandmother did.

I sat on pins and needles, waiting for her response. She stared into me, not at me, but into my being. It felt as if she could see every inch, and I've never felt more exposed. Her eyes narrowing and taking stock of all the little bits and pieces of my soul, parts I had yet to meet myself. When she looked into my eyes, I knew I had been seen, that she somehow knew what I had been witness to in my few short years of existence. It was one of those days where I now felt I could breathe as if I'd been holding my breath for years, just waiting to let it out. I bit back on my lip to keep from crying, I didn't want her to think I was scared, and I definitely didn't want her to believe that I was weak. Truth was, I was elated. Finally, I wasn't alone. I wasn't lost and swirling in this world or stuck believing I was crazy anymore. She had seen me because she too was a witness to the faint memory of those who couldn't let go.

"I guess that depends on what you've seen."

Her response was matter of fact, and she sat back up in her chair, regal and waiting, turning her head just enough to look over at me. Expectantly she sat resolutely in anticipation of my response, that stare where you knew she was reading every thought turning in your mind as you determine if you're going to spill it or attempt the lie first. I'd been waiting for a moment like this, and I wasn't about to waste any time trying to lie to her. I needed her to say it out loud. I needed to stop feeling so isolated in my world filled with all these people trapped around me. Maybe she could tell me what they wanted. Surely, she had come to some conclusion over the years, I was only six, and well, she was well past six.

"I saw her."

As lame as it looks, is as lame as it sounded. Vague wasn't going to work for her, and I knew it, but well, how detailed do you get when you're trying to tell someone that you see some ghost of this unknown teenage girl walking around the house? Did she want to know that her ponytail whipping from side to side made me want to smile? Or did she just want to know that I saw a ghost? I went with the latter option and held my breath.

"Her who? You're going to have to be more specific than that, little girl. Now stop playing games."

My bottom burned at the tone in her voice, and the threat of taking a trip into the backyard was harder to swallow than spitting it all out was going to be, and so it began. I told her everything I had seen up until that point. She listened as I recounted the little girl in the park and Bobby in my closet that one afternoon. She sat and listened to every story I told. Each instance of knowing and even my nightmares. I shared everything. It was as if once I started, I couldn't stop. The stampede of stories plowed through the living room that morning, and she didn't just sit and listen; she heard every word.

For a few days, I couldn't bring myself to leave her side. She and I spent hours talking about the things I had seen, every detail I could remember from any dream I had had the night before, and every story I was told by the lady in my room. It's strange to recount your entire life of six years, especially since you really could only recall the better part of the last two of them. My brother had been born just two days after my fourth birthday, so that first memory of mine was fresh and fairly recent. Let's be honest, most of the things I could recall were more like postcards than any kind of long letter, small snippets of what had happened over days or even months wrapped up in just a couple of lines sent out with some colorful picture attached to it. Here I was sitting in the living room thumbing through them all and telling the story of each image to the woman that would from then on always be my anchor in such things.

I learned how it wasn't only the two of us with the ability to see and know things beyond other's understanding. This had gone on for generations, each woman with a different way of seeing things, each woman with varying degrees of this gift. From what I could tell, my grandmother was stuck with the lion's share, well, as far as we knew then. She not only could see some of the dead walking amongst us, and that great knack of knowing, not just the premonitions of what may come or what once was, but her uncanny ability to see that needle move so franticly when people were lying, but her dreams were legendary with the family. If she was dreaming about you, you paid attention to what she had to say, and if she spent three nights in a row with the same dream, you better believe that's exactly how it was going to happen. That was the gift her mother had as well. My great-grandmother was the real dreamer of the family, though. She'd wake up every morning and write them down. Going back through her journals is almost as if you're reading an account of our family's history. Every single dream she wrote in that book occurred just as written, and she never cared what anyone thought of her gift. If your life had something to do with her dream, you knew it, and it only took one time for you to believe she was crazy and toss it off as some funny dream to learn you'd be better off listening to her. Because then it would happen just as she told you it would. No one ever questioned her once they had seen what it meant to be warned.

That was what most of them were-warnings. It's not as if you could change it much. Of course, there was some degree of control and free will combined with these little tidbits of information, but you had to look for it. It wasn't all set in stone. What most people found was that those moments she gave you ahead of time were just the start of creating some part of a much bigger picture in their lives or the start of one of those crossroad decisions we all have to make over and over again. She'd dream you got a job you didn't know you wanted until she told you about it, but then when the time came, you had just been handed a promotion at your current position. Crossroads. You'd learn of her dream, and with that, you'd have time to think through the things you truly wanted in life, rather than be left with a split-second decision moment. She awarded you an opportunity of clarity, and it was up to you if you chose to take it or not. Many people found that she was not always right, but she was never wrong.

My grandmother grew up around that, and when she started to see things and dream them herself, her mother had already known. She'd seen my grandmother sitting in long discussions with the dead as a girl about my age. It's funny how she had never been afraid of them, but then again, I had never been afraid of them either. Well, other than that one, but I think that one might have even made the hairs on my grandmother's skin perk up in recognition of its hate too. I learned over those few days that my mother and aunt had their own dreams and that those had been the source of knowing when we would be able to escape. My mother had seen it. She had seen him arrive back home that morning, seen him head off to the neighbors that night, and well, my grandmother managed to fill in a few details as well. That's how they had known to be at the back door waiting for us that night. My uncle had already been asked to swing by that morning before he ever had any idea of what was going on within those walls or that we were going to be there.

It felt freeing to be me around her, truly me. I didn't have to hide what I saw, and we soon found that I was surrounded by more ghosts than she was most of the time too. I learned what she already knew about them, that they weren't hanging around with a specific message for someone, they only needed to be heard. They're all just looking for one last release of who they are and what they needed to say, and then they can let go. Sometimes it's funny the things they hold onto, the words that keep them grounded and frozen in place. I recall one that just wanted to talk about their cat. How much they loved and hated it all at the same time, and how much that ball of fur had saved them over the years. I almost wanted to go and adopt one after that. Their sales pitch was incredible, but I somehow managed to refrain from the temptation. At that moment in time anyway.

It all made sense suddenly. Bobby had shown up and told me his story. He had told me what he needed to say, and then poof, he was gone. It's a bit anti-climactic in the grand scheme of things if you think about it, but not all ghosts were just holding on to live in that final chat and then run along to the place they should have been the whole time. Not all of them just needed to be heard. That was evident by my experience with the lady in my room, I had heard her for years, and she hadn't left. I learned that those who had left the living violently tended to stick around much longer. Feeling as if they have more life to live, that their time was cut short, and they still deserve the opportunity to continue on until they choose to let go. Some though, like that anger that haunted our old house, their evil could always be felt, and it was a warning. Those spirits were strong and could do things none of the others could. They could and would hurt you, and the scar across my grandmother's back was more than enough proof for me to steer clear of such things. I only wish I was always capable.

THIRTEEN
Perspective

Where do you go from there? What does a six-year-old do with that kind of information? To say I was a strange child would be too obvious, but it wasn't just my abilities that kept me circling within that microcosm of the weird and unusual. I was a child that grew up way too fast, and it showed. An old soul is what people used to say about me. There was something about the way I saw the world, a bit jaded and maybe even a little bitter if I'm honest with myself, but neither of those words or concepts made any sense to me at the time. I think it was that I never missed anything that was going on around me that threw people off, and well, honestly, it scared them a little bit too. This goes back to learning early on to pay close attention to the body language of another person, to focus in on those little nuances that they can't control as they change moods or focus on a new idea. I see them all.

I've been told by friends and family alike that I can walk into a room full of strangers and, just by looking them over, tell you things about them and their lives that there's no way I could possibly know. Maybe it's part of these gifts I have, or perhaps it is just a survival technique I acquired in those six short years that I've managed to hone throughout the rest of my life. Either way, I have rarely been wrong, which in itself is scary.

I think it's how I knew just what to ask Bobby that day in the closet. I could have said anything, but just looking at his face, I knew what he needed to hear. I've always wondered how people miss those things, but after years of hearing the dead recount the words they need to release, I've learned that people miss way too much from those that they spend the most time around.

You can see it if you pay attention. People watch one day. Sit across from a table of strangers and watch how they interact with each other. Watch how they interact with the other people, and the things around them. I bet you'll be able to tell if they're friends or dating, or possibly even married. Did you notice that look she gave him just out of the corner of her eye with her head down, that slight blush that just barely tinted her chest when she did? Or did you notice how he rummaged in that bag between them without a care in the world or a single consideration for her? So many things that people do that they don't realize they're doing. Every moment of time is just another gift to see each other for who we are and what we want and need. I believe that if we took the time to pay more attention and hear each other, I wouldn't have nearly as many people to listen to after they're gone.

Strange how at six, I could notice these things while others go through life with blinders on and paying attention only to what they find important. This is the best part of anything I've ever been able to do, I think. I sat there with my grandmother and described the ghosts that walked in and out of that house or that were around us when she took me to the park. Not just how they looked, but the parts of them that allowed me to tell her about who they really were. She'd have me explain to her what I thought it was they might need to say before fading away that final time. She'd make me try to distinguish if they were holding on to life longer than they should or if they'd be ready to let go if only given the chance. It was a Master Class on the ins and outs of spirit classification, I guess, and I took volumes of mental notes of every word she said. I learned how wrong I could be, but more often than not, I learned how right I usually was.

My grandmother and I spent weeks, or in truth, it might have been months living every day with those that were no longer living and discussing their existence in death. I guess it's not how most people spend their summer vacations from school, escaping what you thought was a perpetual hell and then talking to dead people. Neither of those were instances I shared with the class that first day of school either. I probably tossed out something along the "I spent the summer with my grandparents" line, which wasn't a lie. In fact, we spent the better part of the next two years with my grandparents. I can't imagine not having that time with them, not learning from them the way I did.

It was my grandmother that showed me what I could do and how this was our normal, and I should never deny it or be ashamed of who I am because of it. But it was my grandfather who showed me who I was. He was a carpenter and spent all of his free time out in the shop he created in their garage. I loved it in there with the smell of sawdust and sweat in a room full of drills, sanders, and massive saws that could remove your entire arm if you made just the wrong move. I spent just as much time in that garage as I did in the living room practically suctioned cupped to my grandmother's hip.

By the end of that first summer, I had my own set of tools to work with and had learned how to properly use every single machine that he had in there. It was magical to watch him work. Seeing the genius that he was. It allowed me to see the brilliance in those that felt compelled by their art and that were blessed with the gift to bring life to something that didn't exist before their hands had an opportunity to see the creation held captive within and release it. I was never very good at that. I could see what it could be, but I wasn't capable of molding it, only seeing it for what it was and it's potential. As much as I thought that made me a failure, he showed me how impossible that thought would always be. In his mind, I could never be a failure as long as I always took the time to try something first. My grandfather had a way of seeing that there was always beauty in the failing, that there was a gift in the mistakes, and that there was always hope for something else in the stumbles. I'd nail a few things together, look at it like it was all wrong and go to pull the nails out, and he'd stop me every time.

"What are you doing?"

The question made me stop and take stock of his carpentry skills for a second. It should have been obvious with me sliding that hammer underneath the head of that nail that I was about to rip it out and start over.

"I'm taking out the nails. I didn't make anything but some wood with nails in it."

He'd just smile down at me. It always just looked like a few pieces of scrap wood that I'd managed to stick together into some odd predicament that they never looked like they belonged in, much less should remain that way. He'd say the same thing every time, and it's the same words I hear anytime I feel like I've just tossed it all together into a mess.

"Well, did you turn it over and look at it from all the angles? You never know; you might find its purpose if you look at it from what you think is the bottom."

Perspective. I might have been having some fun and trying not to hammer my thumb too hard, but that's what he gave me, perspective. Those words have saved me many times from the bottom. Taking the time to look at what I was positive was a complete mess and seeing it for what it really was instead before I ripped it all to pieces and chucked it as some failed attempt. Even in those moments when I took the time and flipped it all around trying to find some purpose for it all and found that it was just a bunch of scrap wood nailed together, I'd see the pieces pulled apart and find something new that could be created from them all now. A nail hole somehow became the eye on what was obviously the head of a duck, and if I flipped this other piece just this way, I could see the tail. There was always a hope for something new, something beautiful in what I had almost written off as a failure.

In his eyes, there was no such thing as failing. Sometimes you made something beautiful with what you had, and sometimes you created something with a purpose that you needed, even if you hammered your thumb a few times in the process. The pain was just a reminder of how hard it just is sometimes to get it right where it needs to be, and as much as your thumb might hurt like hell, you'd see just how important what you made was in the end.

FOURTEEN

The Tree

Those early years in life have so much to do with who we are and what we become. I felt like my place in this world was some secret room where you had to know which book to tilt toward you to be allowed entrance. Fitting into the norm with those around me that were my age, never really existed. My friends and I found plenty of ways to play together but I was not like them in so many ways. Learning early on that playing house with my peers did not encompass any of the same experiences I had known within the walls of my own home growing up. Families were happy, and parents loved each other and didn't hurt each other like mine had. That point of view was changed when we moved into my grandparent's home. They did love each other, and we were all very happy there. But finding 'normal' was hard and not something you just fall into after a start in life like mine had been.

It wasn't the easiest of time, as if any of them had been so far, and the struggles my mother faced as she divorced my father were some she tried hard to keep hidden from my brother and me. No matter how close the storm raged near us, she managed to keep it at bay. Either that or the threat of being pulled out of the house again was enough to keep my father from barreling in and grabbing what he believed he owned in some dark and twisted way. It wasn't long before he gave up trying for a while, and I'm sure whatever or whoever had kept him busy during his long cigarette recovery missions were extra busy and less covert during that time. That little pull of the unknown and what he might do would disappear for brief moments, but they'd always return without prejudice when those true instances of joy actually happened.

My life has never been sunshine, lollipops, and rainbows for too long, but there have been some bright sugar-filled parties here and there. I was the oldest of all the cousins, and they all lived so close that we spent days upon days together. Of course, I spent a lot of that time making sure that the other kids were getting along and having a good time while the adults sat around the table playing cards or dominoes. I enjoyed it, though, in some strange way. I've always been the caretaker type. Watching as others learn to do something new or find the potential within themselves that they had no idea existed. Those were my sunshine moments when I could witness their smiles beam across their faces when everything just clicked. Don't get me wrong, it happened to me too, and I was just as thrilled to experience those moments within myself when they occurred as I was to see them in others.

Maybe it's that I spent so much time with those in the spirit world when they finally found their place, their fulfilled moment, in that release of all they had been holding onto that kept them feeling abandoned or unworthy of who they could have been, that when it happened with the living, it felt as if they could fly. I had some deep hope that those types of experiences would keep them from sticking around to say a few words and to feel heard when it was their time to go. I guess if it were only a matter of listening to one another, that would make it easier on everybody. My grandmother and I wouldn't have had so many to deal with if that were the case. We both knew that they weren't the only ones hanging around, though, and it's the ones that are searching for more of life or that are evil in spirit that would keep us on our toes. It felt like we were always on our toes.

I slept in the front room of that house while we were there, with this beautiful bay window looking out onto the front yard. Well, beautiful during the day, at night, depending on which night, there was much more to be seen than a giant oak tree. That tree was alive in a way that I'm not sure I can explain, but even with the things I had witnessed by that time in my life, something in that tree scared me. I'd try really hard to go to sleep while the adults were still up with the kitchen light on to where I could hear them talking and laughing. They were my sentinels, my guardians of rest, and their loud voices and cackles were a lullaby to me. Those days where they all went to bed early, and I was left there in that front room staring out at that oak tree, I'd watch for any movement within it until my eyelids finally won the battle, capturing me and holding me hostage until morning.

I knew it was out there; it's why I struggled so

much. It felt as if that tree was haunting me, but deep down, I knew it wasn't the tree. There was a darkness out there stalking me just like that van in my nightmares. My cousins would all climb up into the comfort of that tree's big limbs and laugh and play with each other as if nothing were there to hurt them, but it was there. I could feel it. I remember the first week of half-asleep days after tediously watching every leaf shutter in the wind until I couldn't anymore and sitting down to tell my grandmother the things that were keeping me up all night. She, of course, listened. I may have only been a scared little girl, but my boogieman was real; she'd seen them. She sat in quiet contemplation for what felt like an eternity, and I was nervous that she was going to tell me that I was going to have to deal with it on my own, but she didn't. Her only response was one of comfort.

"Don't worry, we'll just have to see what likes to live out there in my tree."

I'm not sure if that sounded comforting to you, but the understanding that this was now a 'we' problem and not a 'me' problem afforded me a moment of respite, a moment of peace. So many times, I had to do things on my own or be the protector, that when the support I needed was always there, I could feel the weight of my world that I had been carrying lighten a little more with every day.

After breakfast, she and I walked out to the tree hand in hand. I couldn't say a word, even if I had wanted to. The shadow of that tree didn't just cloak me from the sun; it held me prisoner with each step. I felt the pressure of its limbs holding me down, and if I didn't know better, I'd had thought I was sinking deeper in quicksand the closer I moved towards the trunk. Each arm reaching out across the yard looking like it would snatch me up and catapult me into the nothingness without remorse at any moment. The closer we crept, the more the fear took hold: that unknowing, that darkness lashing out in hopes of pulling us deeper into it.

I know my grandmother could feel it too. Either that or she was channeling the fear of a shivering six-year-old because each time she'd squeeze my hand, I'd exhale the breath I'd been holding for too long. I didn't notice I wasn't inhaling oxygen like my body required until I was gasping for it with each reminder pumped into my little hand by her own. No matter how scared I felt, I knew she had me, and we were there to investigate this ominous tree together. I didn't think anything could hurt me if she was there next to me, it wouldn't dare.

I think in the back of my mind, I had hoped we would have found some ghost there hiding in the shadow that just needed to be heard. Then all of my problems would be solved, and I'd be whisked off into a dreamland full of gumdrops and candy-filled rivers that night, and the tree would just be a tree. It was wishful thinking and a child's dream, and it wasn't going to be the case. When she finally reached out and placed her hand against the heart of the tree, I thought it would swallow her whole, and I whimpered despite myself when she made contact with it. Being connected to her connected me to that tree as well. The darkness within screaming in the hallows of my mind and wailing in pain. It was almost as if the tree was begging for its own release from the anger that had taken up residence without permission.

I'm not sure how long we stood there or how

ridiculous we must have looked in the front yard holding hands and touching a tree, but it was almost a second too long before she stepped back, and the screaming stopped flooding my thoughts. I don't think I could have lasted any longer than I did, the sounds of pain already being boxed up and shoved into one of those hidden storage rooms in hopes that it would never be needed again. Of the things we try to forget in our lives, they are always the ones that find a way to escape when we least expect it, and I didn't want this moment finding its way loose ever again.

My grandmother stood up to her full height and faced that tree, almost as if she were staring it down and daring it to reach for her. I was mesmerized by her strength and couldn't pull my eyes from her, and for a moment, the fear was gone. She looked down at me, nodded matter of factly, and directed each of our steps back toward the house like she had solved all the problems of the universe and was on her way to reward herself with ice cream.

It's exactly what we did. Vanilla with sprinkles.

FIFTEEN

The Darkness Within

After every brightly colored piece of candy had found its way into my mouth, she picked up our bowls and tried to explain. I think I had an understanding before the first words fell past her lips, but to hear her tell it only made it more real. I had been dreaming of that darkness for years now. It had stalked me and threatened to pull me into oblivion too many times to not recognize it now. The shrill screaming of the tree seeping out of that hidden box for a split second. I knew what it was out there waiting for me, and I was petrified.

The unknown had found me, had followed me, and no longer only crept throughout my nightmares, but it taunted me nightly in the form of that tree. The reminder that it was always just within reach tore into my sense of safety. Instead of the looming fear of my father, I was stalked by a behemoth that couldn't move from where it was rooted, but it inched closer to me every night.

I don't know how long she tried to explain it to

me, but I understood it more than I think even she realized. I was destined to be haunted by this darkness forever. I was never going to be able to escape its torment, and I'd live surrounded by its shadow for the rest of my life. What a doom and gloom thing to learn at the age of six. It's as if the world looked over and said, "Look, little girl, we know you have your whole life ahead of you, and well, it hasn't been all that great so far, but meet your new companion from here on out. Good luck!" Whatever happened to giving me a teddy bear that I'd cherish for the rest of my life and would still have on a shelf in my room as I lay on my deathbed, still watching over me and filling me with loving memories? Nope, not me. I get an ominous and evil darkness following me around and watching my every move. If that doesn't give you pause for a moment, nothing really will.

I spent the rest of the day sitting in front of that window and staring at that tree. Trying to formulate some escape plan, but how far can you really get when you're just a little girl. As I sat there, I knew there was no getting away from it in the end. I'd come up with plans on how to try and get it to leave. Maybe I could not be seen by the tree for a while, and it'll think I've gone. Where even would its eyes be anyway? It's a tree. It's not like I could blindfold it and play hide and seek until it got tired and quit playing, walking home with its head down all defeated when it was over. I was going to have to stand up to it and let it know that I wasn't going to let it win. That's pretty damn hard for a little girl. How many nights do you have to face the boogieman before he stops being scary? Way too many.

We were in that house with my grandparents for almost two years, and for almost two years, that darkness kept me company. Even when I would sleep in another room, and that tree wasn't swaying me into my restless sleep, I could feel it close. Sometimes I felt as if it would slowly start to seep through the walls and consume the room just like it did in my dream, erasing the stairs one by one until there was nothingness surrounding me, and I'd just disappear. Falling headfirst into the unknown, what a nightmare. There it was, my biggest fear staring me right in the face every day for two years.

I didn't let it control me, I couldn't, and every few weeks or so, when I could feel it getting stronger, I'd catch my grandmother outside face to face daring it to try anything. She was my guardian against the darkness, and she'd give up every ounce of light she had to stand between me and its power. It's how she came to have that scar across her back that no one ever asked her about, but I knew the story. She had stood against her own darkness and had the battle scars to prove it.

She had been about fifteen or so, and it was the first time she noticed something was off. Her older brother had been acting strange, and she couldn't quite put her finger on it. Her mother had been out of town for about a week, and taking that into account, it's likely the reason any of this happened in the first place. I was told that he looked as if he hadn't slept in days. Dark circles deep under his bloodshot eyes, and there was something sluggish about his walk. She said he didn't say a word; he just grabbed her and threw her into a shelf. Stunned by it all, she wasn't sure how to respond. Do you attack your brother or try to talk to him after something like that?

I would have lost it and gone ballistic had it

been me, but well, it was a different time, and it wasn't me. She could see something was wrong, and she could see that he wasn't himself. It's when he came at her the second time that it happened. Like a rag doll, he picked her up and tossed her into a window. It shattered on contact, and one of the edges sliced her open about eight inches across her back. In true Mighty Mouse form, my great grandmother returned to see her collide with the glass and ran over to help. Her hands were covered in blood as my grandmother lay there bleeding. None of this mattered to him, and he went to attack her again but was met with his mother's hand covered in his sister's blood instead. She smeared it across his face as he leaned down to grab at her one more time, to finish what he had started. The second her hand left his face, he stopped. There was no explanation for it, no reasoning that makes any sense as to what happened at that moment, but it was over as quickly as it had begun.

My grandmother was obviously alright, and it never happened to her again. As wonderful as it sounds to not have to deal with what was haunting me, I was in no hurry to stand up and try to fight it physically. I might have had a lot of attitudes, but that doesn't translate into physical strength by any means. If it did, I'd be able to lift tanks with one hand for fun. As it were, I could barely keep my butt out of trouble and free from those wisteria switches and my grandmother's accurate swing.

SIXTEEN

Moving On

Like I said, we lived with my grandparents for about two years. My brother and I spending sporadic moments with our father, but they lessened more and more as time went on. I think the knowledge that he not only was responsible for us the entire time we were with him but that he was unable to control my mother any longer with us as pawns cut too much into his drinking time. We became a nuisance and found ourselves with several random women watching us during those visitations. Not that they did anything, most of the time, they were just as drunk and high as my father was. He became a few moments in time pushed back into memories that barely resonate when I think about those years.

He wasn't the tornado I had been a witness to for so long when we went to visit but became more of a flash flood. An event with little warning, and although most everything came out of it unscathed, the landscape had been changed, and there was always some damage somewhere, even if the majority of it was on the inside where most people never noticed if they didn't dig around a bit. Every couple of months, there'd be a flash flood warning, and sometimes not a drop of rain would fall, and other times, the bottom fell out of the sky. Most children are thrilled to know they're going to spend some time with their estranged parent. I was ecstatic when he would just forget us altogether. It was always a coin toss, though, and I never knew if it would end up pouring or not.

It was about a year after our escape that my mother began dating again, not that she really ever said that's what she was doing, but I noticed. She deserved some time to enjoy herself, those brief moments of freedom from us, and an hour or two to forget all of the pain she had endured for so long. To say she was reticent is probably an understatement, but she was also young and lonely. Just in her mid-twenties, there was a lot of life and love still to experience for her. Now, I'm not sure how many men she may have dated, but one quickly became a regular, and the fact that my grandparents knew who he was and approved of him said a lot. He didn't come alone, though. He was already completely wrapped around the finger of another. Of course, she was three with freckles and a smile as big and toothy as my brothers. In fact, side by side at that age, they looked as if they could have been twins.

I don't remember my mom dating him or him being around too often, I'm sure he was, but I'd be lying if I said I had kept any of those memories around. The first real memory of meeting him I had was going to this newly turned three-year-old's birthday party at one of those kid traps with games and prizes and the dreaded ball pit. I think they were allowing the three of us an opportunity to see how well we got along in our natural habitat. I mean, if kids can't be friends with each other in their pizza and sugar-filled church with a robotic mouse leading the worship band, it was never going to happen. It was the perfect plan. Our first memory together would always be one of the happiest, it was pure genius on their part. Not that they were attempting to manipulate anything, but you can't help but think if there isn't a spell cast upon children as they walk through the doorway of places like that, or if it's somehow filled with some pheromone that only affects kids twelve and under. Either way, the three of us became fast friends, especially her and my brother. They were only six months apart, and their ankle-biter cuteness multiplied exponentially when they were together, and they used every bit of that to their full advantage. I couldn't really blame them; I would have too, but they would use it against me as well, and I somehow managed to be talked into playing some of the weirdest and imaginative games every time we were together.

There's something about single parents that puts them into a different mindset when they're dating. I've heard it likened to an audition or interview process, and well both my mother and her new suitor were single parents. They were no exception to this need to ensure that not only were their hearts safe, and for my mother, was her face safe, but they needed to make sure that us kids weren't going to be tossed into something that could break us any more than we already were. It's one thing to be taken out of a situation where you're not secure, even if you do have love for that person, it's another to rip children from each other that have created a bond like siblings do. They couldn't deny that they loved each other and wanted to be together, though, and just before I turned eight, I had a new dad and that sister I had wanted just a few years earlier when my brother decided to show up instead. I don't know how, but in an instant, our family was complete, and it felt the way it always should have been.

I can remember the first couple of years with the three of us in one room, always together and always playing. We played like brothers and sisters and boy did we fight like brothers and sisters too. In this newly created family, I found peace and joy, and I no longer feared my father coming to take me away. In fact, he had moved away, and we barely heard from him. Maybe a phone call on our birthday or at Christmas, and a couple of summers, my brother and I spent a week or two with him wherever he might have been at the time, but knowing I was going home and the happiness that looked like created the levee I needed to keep the floodwaters from creating too much damage each time I saw him. It's strange how those who know how to manipulate know just how to make you feel guilty for their shortcomings and inabilities to do the things they should have done. My father was one such person, and that was the pain I struggled with each time we returned home- guilt. For what, I can't tell you. I think I thought I was supposed to love him more and spend more time with him and try harder to see him and talk to him. It took me a long time to realize that it was not my job but his. Even with that epiphany, it took a while to release that misplaced guilt.

Those first couple of years were also strangely quiet for me. I rarely saw a ghost, and that darkness that had found a home in the tree had not been able to get to me again either. When we'd stop in to visit my grandparents, I could still feel it there, and each time it seemed as if the roots had lifted further out of the ground in an attempt to escape its earthly bonds. My grandmother couldn't have cared less about it either. Once we moved out, she ignored it as if she had never acknowledged its existence in the first place. I still kept away from it though, as happy as I was, I didn't want to tempt giving over the joy I had found by tempting fate. The tree was still there, and the darkness was still trapped, and if I wasn't careful, the sound of it wailing would echo in my mind and bounce off the walls there like an empty ballroom, and for a second, I'd remember the fear. Then I'd remember that it no longer had a home here, or so I thought.

SEVENTEEN

The Big Move

For years the world seemed normal. Well, as normal as it could be for someone like me. Trauma holds onto you no matter how much joy you find. The true escape from the pain is to open it up and let yourself find the bits of happiness that were hidden within. To remind yourself that the abuse was done to you and not because of you. That's a hard realization to make sometimes, and one I wish fewer people had to learn. Sadly, it's one some of us are forced to endure over and over again.

I was happy and content with life, and at times I experienced more joy than I thought possible or that I felt I deserved. Such a crazy concept to consider as a nine-year-old-contentment. We stayed close to my grandparents for a few years, and then as life often does, things changed. Led by my dad's job, we were forced to move out of the area and to a place I had already known all too well. The thought of returning to that small town just on the eastern side of the pine curtain was not my idea of a good move at all, and I was petrified.

My mother didn't seem that excited about it either, there were a lot of tough memories waiting there for her, and no matter how disconnected she might have been from my father, she was still dragging a caravan of pain and hurt behind her with every step. Pain like that is forgotten for a time when you're sitting in happiness, but when it's time to get up and move around in life, we feel that tug all too quickly. The fear returns, and you can taste it coating your mouth in bitterness and tainting the sweetness you had enjoyed just moments earlier. She did a good job of trying to hide it, she was an expert on doing so, but if you paid close enough attention, you could see her face twist at the taste of that fear returning. One I thought I had learned to forget, only to find the flavor was one I remembered all too well right along with her.

I had to have been in the fourth or fifth grade when we packed up our blended family and headed into what I thought were the trenches of hell. A world filled with pain, fear, and too many ghosts. The ghosts of my past haunting my mind, but the ghosts of that house felt awakened somehow as we drove closer to our new home. As we pulled into the drive smack in the middle of a dead-end street, I knew this was the end of the new normal I had found and that those few years were only a vacation from before, and all of that was now over.

Waiting for the other shoe to drop is an expression I feel to my core at times. Watching as it dangles there on the end of a finger, swaying back and forth. Always knowing it's going to fall and hit the ground and holding my breath with each movement. A hostage to the fear, held by the unknown, by the inevitable. I tried for the first few weeks to enjoy myself, meet all the new neighbor kids and play around in the backyard. It was fun, but I could feel that darkness looming and gathering itself closer with each day. It may have been held in place for the last few years by those roots, but the miles between us only pulled that rubber band tighter until finally, it was able to slingshot itself in my direction.

Funny how the first place I remember encountering it is the one place that was able to pull it back towards me. As if my feet touching the ground there called it to me, rekindled our twisted connection, and brought us swiftly back together somehow.

It had to have been summer when we settled into our home there on Home Street. How someone found it appropriate to make a dead-end street a place to call Home, I don't understand. Not the title I might have given it, but for the moment, I suppose it was ours. The three of us were out exploring the area as kids often do, and being new to our surroundings, there was plenty to explore. The road ended at a forest full of adventures just waiting to be found, and we were not immune to its siren call. Pine needles everywhere. We sounded like an army traipsing through those woods. The games of hide and seek and the dreams of treehouses and secret forts bringing us there almost daily during the heat of that year.

As much as I tried to have fun, and don't get me wrong, I had a blast; I could feel something stalking me at times. A shadow sliding across the ground out of the corner of my eye, an extra tree branch snapping in the distance, or a sudden chill across my neck when it was well over ninety degrees outside.

I knew it was there, and it reveled in its taunting of me. I had grown accustomed to the freedom from the fear for too long. Feeling it again was more than overwhelming, and it would make me physically ill at times. The stress of it taking over my body, causing me to find a way to function, wound up so tight I knew I might snap at any second.

I tried to play it off for a while, to convince myself that I was just being a scared little girl over some show or movie I had seen on television that triggered these thoughts. I almost started to believe it until the dream. That very first night when we moved in, I remember those stairs disappearing around me once again. I knew I was no longer going to be left alone by any of it, and I was right. This was my Welcome Home party, whether I had accepted the invite or not.

The darkness had followed me, and it felt as if I dreamt of it nearly every night after that. Its continued efforts to pull me deep into its despair and surrounding me in fear were constant. I couldn't escape it, and I tried everything I could to hide from it, but it's difficult to stop a nightmare. It's even more difficult when that nightmare stalks you whether you're asleep or not. It felt like trying to catch smoke with my fingers, you can see it there, but you can't seem to get hold of it no matter what you do. The wisps slipping between your fingers no matter how tightly you try to grab at it.

That was how my life felt for many years, like a magic trick. You could see the moving parts, but the trick was hiding all of the difficult moves from the rest of the world. They didn't want to see any of that anyway. They wanted to see the smoke and mirrors and the fun. I believe we all do this, but honestly, it's likely my distorted understanding of the reality I knew and not how the rest of the world experiences it. Just another reminder that I don't play happy family like the rest of the kids, but I learned to adapt. That should be my descriptive word, the one at the top of the list when people ask about my best qualities. Well, I can adapt to damn near anything. How does your world look? I'll let you know where I can fit in; just give me a minute. The kid version of a chameleon, or as one of my friends would say, super Gumby. It's not a trait I've given up over the years; it's just one I don't allow to lead out the gate. I gathered up many more amazing qualities of my own during those years that get top billing these days, and I plan to keep it that way.

EIGHTEEN

Emma

I woke the next morning to the sound of some little girl muttering to herself as she played in my room. She couldn't have been more than five or six, and she would never grow to be any older than that either. I spent the day ignoring her, thinking I could just forget she was there and pretend that I didn't see her. Maybe that would keep me from seeing any of the others too. I knew it wouldn't, but I was willing to take the chance that it might for at least a day or two. My welcome was instantaneous, with barely a breath between arriving and being tossed back toward the edge of the veil. Want it or not, I knew I didn't have a choice in the matter either. Living my life with those who no longer had one was again my reality, and I nearly stomped my foot in frustration. Why couldn't I just enjoy being a kid? Was the last couple of years all I had earned? Either way, here I was again, sharing space with the dead, and this time she was in my room.

However, I had learned long ago that if you didn't

acknowledge them, they would never know you were there. It's like a switch that flips on when you look straight into the face of a ghost or address them in conversation. This is the reason my grandmother spent her days sitting in a chair pretending to do anything but see the ghosts that found their way into her presence. She was who I aspired to be someday, and I thought I could do the same. I was wrong. That kind of skill comes with experience and dedication, something I was still working to gain.

I should have known with how observant children can be that she'd notice me noticing her all too easily. I might have made it a few hours, and I think all of those were only because I wasn't in the room with her. It was a lazy day and raining outside, so running off into the woods and away from the kindergarten ghost was not in the cards. My sister and I shared a room, and she wanted to play forts or Barbies or tea party or likely all of the above all at once. We were overachievers and multitaskers and really good at excelling at both. It would not have been unheard of for us to build a fort, set it up with a tea party and play Barbies at the same time, either way, I remember the blankets deftly pulled tight from bed to bed and tied skillfully into what was a fort large enough for our entire family and well, a little ghost girl too.

My sister had run off to gather up some more "tea" and to sneak some cookies as well for us to enjoy during our arduous play schedule, and I was left alone. I have a fair imagination, but it's always put to better use when others are participating. Without their push to keep the story going, I quickly spiral into my own thoughts and space. This is where she found me. I sat there with my mind off in thought of who could this little girl be, why was she suddenly in my room, and would I or did I want to help her? In that field of questions, I was caught looking directly at her. I didn't even realize I had been until she looked up at me and our eyes met. By then, it was too late, and I was trapped by her knowing she had been seen. What could a kid this age have left to say? Why was she holding on still? Whatever it was, I was about to find out.

It wasn't lost on me that she was about the same age as my brother and sister were at the time, and entertaining and listening to two five-year-old's was already enough, but adding one that never needed to sleep to the mix, that was a whole different level of entertaining. I quickly looked away, hoping that she really didn't see me or that she could brush it off as a coincidence, but I knew that was not about to happen. My face twisted at the idea of it all, and my heart sank at the first word.

"Hey!"

Dammit! Trying to pretend that I was just going about my business and playing again, I started talking to myself and my toys. Turning to face her and shout out for my sister to hurry up, surely that will make her think I didn't see her after all.

Leaning in and pushing her face close to mine, I flinched, and she saw it.

"Heeeyyy!!"

Defeated, I exhaled into my lap and knew where there's one, there will always be more, and I was tossed back into what was my true reality in an instant.

"HHHHeeeeeeeyyyyyyyy!"

This was not going away. Having a younger brother and sister, I knew she would only get louder and more annoying with each try. I was trapped again, and I made a vow that day that as soon as I could escape this little town, I would never ever ever ever live here again. With a sigh, I responded and hoped my sister continued to take her time while I figured out what exactly I had just fallen into.

"What? You don't have to be so loud; you know."

My eyes rolled so far to the back of my head; I swear I could see brain matter. This was not how I had planned to spend today nor any day for that matter, but here I was tossed into their world, that place between the living and the dead once more. Well, isn't that just great?

I could have thought of a thousand other things I would have liked to happen to me before starting my first day at a new school and becoming the new best friend of a little girl that no one else could see was nowhere near the top of that list at all. She was just as fun and annoying as my brother and sister were, only she had an expectation of getting attention no matter who might be around. As awkward as I might have been as a kid, talking to what equated to an imaginary friend in everyone else's eyes at the age of nine was a bit too weird even for me. Regardless of what I thought or wanted, from that first moment on, she followed me everywhere, and I mean everywhere.

Nothing was sacred to her, and I spent a good five minutes explaining as quietly as possible that following me into the bathroom was not going to work for me. So instead, she stood outside of the door waiting and asking a million questions while she did. I couldn't turn her off, and the only break I did get from her was when I closed my eyes to go to sleep. If I could have figured out a way to sleep forever, you could have called me Sleeping Beauty and told Prince Charming to just leave me the hell alone; I didn't need waking. Unfortunately, that was never going to be the case, and I was going to have to learn how to deal with her on my own.

Her name was Emma. I know this because not only did she tell me, she spelled it out for me many, many times. Emma, E-M-M-A, had lived a few houses down who knew how many years ago and had apparently become very ill and died. It must have been while she slept because she didn't remember it at all. The only thing she could tell me was that she remembered her mother reading her a bedtime story, and then when she woke up, no one could hear her. She tried for a long time until they left, and another family moved into the house. They didn't have any kids, so when she noticed us on the street, she decided our house was as good as any to be ignored in, but at least she'd be able to see all the fun new toys we had. She liked chasing around our dog too. Which explained a lot about her strange behavior there the last couple of weeks, running around the house barking her head off for no apparent reason. My mother almost lost her mind trying to get that dog to settle down, and apparently, seeing my mother get frustrated was just as entertaining to Emma as chasing the dog had been.

She was a whirlwind of energy that never needed recharging, and I was her new outlet. I had overheard a few stories between our neighbor and my parents and found out that Emma had been dead for about three years, and so she had three years' worth of questions to get through by the time she met me. Our house was right across the street from the elementary school, too, so to say Emma didn't have her share of fun during that time would be wrong. Little kids tend to see spirits more easily than adults do, so the kindergarten teachers were a bit more than troubled at the announcement from several munchkins in their classroom that Emma was bothering them. Especially since they had all known Emma and been there when she died just a few years earlier.

They never knew what to believe, and I think most adults shrug it off to the idea of an imaginary friend, but when you have four kids in the same class yelling that it really was Emma telling them to make weird noises, it's a little bit more difficult to just let it go. She knew better than to try and convince me to do silly things during classes, but it didn't make her constant talking and questions any less annoying. There were too many times when she was around that I looked like I had lost my mind and started talking to myself. Each time report cards were handed out, mine said the same thing for every class, "Talks too much." That would have been fine, and I would have owned it if I wasn't being forced to talk. It's not as if I wasn't trying to pay attention.

She went everywhere I did, like a lost little puppy dog, and after a while, I treated her the same as I did my own brother and sister. When she had questions, I'd answer them as best as I could, and when she was annoying, I'd yell at her to leave me alone. Which worked about as well as it did with the other two, which is to say not very well at all. She would disappear from time to time, and just as I could, there was no doubt that she felt that darkness when it was near. Many times, I noticed the shadows or get that uneasy feeling, she'd vanish for hours, and when it was really bad, sometimes I wouldn't see her for days.

I began to worry that if she was that scared of the darkness, could it also hurt her, or was this a little girl scared of the boogieman? I was just a little girl scared of the boogieman, and I didn't have my grandmother here to stand in front of me this time. I was going to have to learn how to deal with this one on my own because no matter how much I didn't want it to be true, I knew that it was tethered to me indefinitely. Pretending like it didn't exist was baseless and only going to delay the inevitable acceptance.

After several weeks of her being around, it was odd to go days without seeing her when she'd disappear. Although it would have been nice to ship my siblings off with her every once in a while, five and six-year-olds can be annoying when you're the big sister trying to live your life at nine. No, that's wrong. Siblings of that age are some of the biggest pains in the asses. They're still asking a thousand questions a day; they think they know everything and are grown enough to do it all. When they realize they can't, they are capable of toddler-sized tantrums. They are overwhelming and yet love the crap out of you more and more each day. They can also hate you furiously when they get mad at you, and it's a razor's edge the life you lead in their presence. That whole "family is forever" motto can seem like a life sentence some days.

This was also the case with Emma. She had quickly grown attached to me and adopted me as her own big sister. This really was great, and I was honored. You don't usually get to choose your family, but in this instance, she did, and that family was me. However, I knew, even if she didn't, at some point, she was going to have to go where she should have disappeared to from the beginning. How do you explain or convince a child that they don't belong there with you after they've latched onto your life? She knew her parents weren't dead, so I couldn't tell her they would be waiting, and really, I wasn't sure how to get her to the place she needed to be in order to move on anyway. I'd never had to show someone how it was done, only sit and listen to their stories, to their fears and then watch as they faded from our world and were realized in whatever afterlife there might be. I hadn't seen it. I couldn't describe it to her or play off like it would be a fun trip to an amusement park full of giant lovable mice or anything. I was out of my depth, but the longer she stuck around, the more real this non-life became for her, and I could see it holding her hostage to a nonexistence and making the goal to move on harder and harder. I didn't want to see her trapped here. As much as she might have been a pain in my ass, she didn't belong, and she needed to find her way to where she was going. She needed to start her real adventure.

I had tried to talk to her about it a few times with no success, and it was going to take a miracle to make her understand. Have you ever tried to explain to a wall why it's a wall and the reason it belongs where it is? It felt a lot like that, only this wall had a lot more questions than I had answers. I didn't know how I was going to figure it out, but I couldn't leave Emma here forever. I wouldn't allow her to become a waif of a being flitting in and out of existence for eternity. So, I did the only thing a girl like me could think of; I called for reinforcements.

NINETEEN

A Mother's Touch

I guess the first thought is that I would have called my grandmother, but well, this was a world in which long-distance phone charges were a real thing, and those phone companies docked you by the minute. You know, ancient times, before cellphones and when the only form of communication was a landline or smoke signals, and I wasn't allowed to play with matches. Before you get all excited, no, there were no dinosaurs that roamed the earth while I was a child, other than the librarian at my school. She may have very well been a mummy raised from the dead for all I know. She definitely looked like one. Come to think of it, there were no computers in people's homes either. Maybe they were still building the pyramids while I was in elementary school, but probably not. Let's just say it was a while ago, but not that long ago. Not really, well, maybe. Anyway.

I should be honest and say that she was my first choice, but well, I'm not sure she would have done as wonderfully as my partner in crime did. It took me a few days to figure it out, and as a child of nine, I feel like I came up with the idea perfectly. Actually, I didn't come up with any idea, but I'm taking credit because this is my story, and we all need to be the hero of our own story every now and again. Of course, I didn't know what was going to work, and I tried a thousand different other things first. I went down that laundry list of ideas I had already mentioned but trying to convince Emma that moving on would turn out more fun for her than staying and playing with me and the other little kids at school that could see her was never going to work. She was having too much fun. I needed to find her a reason, so I looked for what would have been my own. If I had died right then, my consciousness clinging to the life I had, what would give me the power to let go? For that's what it truly is, right? The power within ourselves to see that there is hope in growing, in letting go of what we thought was important to find what might be waiting on the other side of the fear. To find the courage to exist in the manner in which we were created to, to embrace our path and step forward. That's a lot to muster up for a five-year-old, or so I thought.

It had been days of trying to reason with this child, and I was just about to give up and resolve to the idea of growing old with Emma following me forever. That was until I was walking through the house, frustrated out of my being at arguing with her, and I noticed my mother watching me. She half smirked, and I think I heard her giggle a few times at my stamping through the kitchen and huffing and puffing like I was going to blow my top like a tea kettle. I'm sure I was a sight and a half, but it only frustrated me more. I grabbed a snack and flung myself up to the dining table and pouted for a good minute or two before she grabbed a glass of water and joined me.

"Troubles, little one?"

I groaned and rolled my eyes. She knew how much I hated being called that. I was the oldest and grown enough not to be called "little one." Emma knew it too, and as she stood at the corner of the table next to me, armed with a thousand more questions, I was sure of it, and she started laughing. Now, I knew my mother was more than capable of understanding what I might be dealing with; she wasn't ignorant to my abilities, even if she and I had never really discussed them. It wasn't as if she could be of too much help for me not seeing the muted population that most other people ignored as well. She left my understanding and most questions for my grandmother. I have to conclude that the two of them had several conversations about me while we lived there with them, but looking back, my mother and I barely even recognized it. I think she had hoped like I did, that after the last couple of years, I had maybe grown out of them, but when you're watching your kid talk to themselves for the better part of a day with no one else around, that hope becomes more of a lost cause than anything else. Emma had been following me for months, and it's been established that I'm not nearly as stealthy as I'd like to believe I am.

"I'm almost ten and older than all of them, don't call me little one. They're the little ones. Not me!"

Frustration quickly turned into anger, and I just wanted to hide in my closet in the dark and quiet for a while, but there was no chance of respite with Emma around, and I'd already been locked in a closet with a ghost once. That was not something I felt I needed to experience again, nor would it have fulfilled my need for quiet or the freedom from a perpetual companion I hadn't asked for. It would have been different if she had been a dog instead, then I could have enjoyed all of the fun and none of the mess a real puppy would have created, but here we were, and I was done. Months pass like years when you don't have anything more pressing to accomplish than your math worksheets, and Emma had been attached to my hip for what felt like a hundred years. It was likely closer to about five or six months if I try and piece together that year enough.

"How about you start paying rent, and then you can tell me what to call you? Until then, you're stuck with it."

She smiled down at me as I huffed again. Those were trying times in my life, those years between birth and adulthood. I'd been tossed into a world that required me to develop cunning, wit, and survival skills from the very beginning. I rarely thought like the other kids, and I definitely didn't see the world the same way most other kids did either. I hated being treated like one too. It's hard when you look nine, but mentally and emotionally, you felt like you'd already lived a lifetime. Being a kid can be hard. My life as a kid was excruciating. She waited until I settled back into my snack and asked me again.

"What's the matter with you today? You're huffin' and puffin' all over the house like you're related to the Big Bad Wolf and gettin' ready to seek revenge on the three little pigs."

Whipping my head up, confused, I watched as

she leaned down and blew my half-empty bag of crackers across the table. There was no way to stop from laughing at it all, and as frustrated as I might have been, I'm not sure I had considered blowing anyone's house down until that moment. And if I had thought it might work to send Emma on her way, I'd had probably tried it. We giggled for a bit, and she'd egg it on by poking or tickling me here or there, and by the time we were done, I had giggled away enough frustration to talk about it. The first question that came to mind was the one I had been searching for on my lists of things to try and had just forgotten to write down.

"What would you do if I died?"

I didn't realize until much later in life that this is the one question no parent wants to think about, much less discuss with anyone. It's like saying Macbeth in the theater. It isn't done. It all seems filled with bad luck, and no parent ever wants to toss that thought out into the universe. Leave it to my mother to push past it and try to navigate her way through to an answer. She pulled her hands together on the table in front of her and released a breath of what I can only guess was pain and fear, and when she looked at me again, there was hurt behind her eyes. An unimaginable hurt that finds its way to the surface when you think of such atrocities.

"That's a difficult question to answer, and not one I'm especially happy to think about. The truth is, a part of me would die too. There's a piece of me that always belongs to you, and you'd have to hold onto it for me until we were together again, and I'd never be whole without it."

She held my eyes with hers by some invisible thread, and I knew how hard it had been for her to think about it. What I concluded many years later was how often she must have considered not only the mortality of my brother and me but hers as well. There's a lot of thinking that happens between the raised hand and its forward trajectory towards your face, and none of it good. There's a difference between being forced to contemplate the thought and when force is used to create the thought. Those types of thoughts had been birthed inside of her on countless occasions. I try not to think about all the things she had to have gone through during that time, just as much as I tried not to think about my own time in captivity with a madman either.

At that moment, I forgot about Emma. That message was for me, regardless of what she thought she was helping with when she came to sit down, and it was one that stayed with me every day after. Part of me sustained my mother, and she needed me as much as I needed her. One unable to breathe without the other, and it only solidified how the two of us kept each other alive for those years full of pain and terror.

The air in the room disappeared for a moment, but it all returned with the smile she gave me before lifting me out of the chair to hug me. After she let go and walked away from the table, I turned to look over at Emma, but she was gone. I thought maybe she had just disappeared bored by the conversation and went to go and find something else to occupy her time until she could start in on the never-ending questions and talking she seemed to manage.

When I returned to my room, she wasn't there.

I waited around for days, expecting to see her pop into the room or wake me with a question, but I never saw Emma again after that day there at the dining table. She didn't need to tell me goodbye. She needed to go home. My mother's words were a beacon that reached out to the little girl and showed her how tethered we all are to each other. I knew Emma only wanted to be with her family again and realizing that if she didn't go to the place she needed to be to wait for them, she would never get that opportunity. It took a few days, but in the end, I was happy for her.

I still think of Emma every now and again. I wonder if she's found her family yet or if she's still waiting, standing vigil as the welcome party for those that she loves. She makes me hope that someday she might be waiting to greet me there as well. Of all the companions I've had through this life, she is the one I've always missed the most. I might even let her follow me into the bathroom running off a thousand questions if I could find another hour with her. She was, after all, the family that chose me, if only for a moment.

TWENTY

New School

Emma might have been the first to stick around like that, but she wasn't going to be the last. I spent way too many years followed by unwanted guests, new friends, and what turned out to be countless lessons in life learning from the dead's mistakes and regrets.

So many left just needing to be heard, with those thoughts and feelings eating them up even in death. It put me in a position to always try to say what I mean and feel. Let's face it, what could I have genuinely learned if, when it all was said and done, I end up just like them. Lost in regret and words unsaid. I couldn't do that to me or someone like me either.

I can recount several of them from across the years, but Emma was the first one that attached herself to me and my life. It was bittersweet when she was gone. I lost a friend that day or, more accurately, a sibling. She had become my third little ankle-biter, following me around asking thousands of questions and annoying the hell out of me, just like the breathing ones did. I was glad she had found her home, but it meant I was the only one left that could feel what was stalking me. I was the only one there when I woke in the night from the nightmares. Once again, it was me alone with the darkness.

Those dreams kept me trapped for years with no escape. Swaying back and forth through a world of fear and unknowing. I couldn't put my finger on it, but it felt as if the more time went on, the more I understood it. Maybe it was my maturity that helped me to feel what it was a little clearer. I'm not really sure. It became an intimate part of my life, entangled in my being. After a few years, I was less afraid and saw it more as a daily companion. I couldn't let the fear determine my life. I had hardly allowed that to happen when what I was truly afraid of was in the same room with me and more real.

I think my lack of fear weakened it over the years, but there were still the nightmares, and the truth of those petrified me. I knew it was there, and those dreams would wake me into a terror I couldn't escape, and those were the nights I knew better than to go back to sleep. I didn't want to fall victim to the never-ending dream sequence that was waiting for me behind my eyelids. I took control of what I could, and it made it bearable to a point. I could function knowing it couldn't keep me hostage forever, not while I had any say in the matter.

As for that old house full of ghosts, it slipped into half a memory. My life existed on that dead-end street, and in those woods, for the few years, we lived there. My mother was careful to avoid that side of town, and I don't think she ever found herself on that road again after she drove away from it all those years ago. Her own ghosts and demons were still locked up behind those walls, and she was unwilling to tempt them towards her.

I know she struggled while we were back there, nightmares ripping their way through her happiness, trying to take hold of the life she now knew. They'd grab at her every once in a while, but she'd fling them off just as quickly as they latched on. Nothing can control you if you don't allow it the time it needs to burrow into your thoughts, and she snatched away the shovel every time. That's not to say there aren't a few divots here and there where they tried, and some I'm sure she's filled back in, but we never escape without a few scars, even if you can't see them.

Life existed differently for me there after Emma left. Nestled in my little corner of the world, I didn't see too many ghosts after that, and I was grateful for our seclusion. That's not to say they didn't show up every now and again, but they were the easy ones, and I learned how to listen to them and go about my life at the same time living back in that small town. It was as if I found my rhythm there, and by the time we were ready to move a few years later, I was almost able to function like a normal person. At least I was able to create the appearance of functioning like a normal person anyway.

Then there was middle school. Nothing and no one is normal in middle school, especially when you're the new kid, and I was always the new kid. My parents did a great job of trying to keep us from having to move so much, but during that three-year time span, their attempts were an utter failure. We even moved ten houses down from the one we were renting once because the owners sold it, which put us one house away from the school district I had been attending and smack dab on the other side and into a completely different one. One house, and here I was tossed into another school, again.

Middle school is hard on most kids but be the weird nerdy kid that sees ghosts and knows way more than she should. Oh, and be the new kid too. That's a winning combination if I ever knew one. Good thing I learned to master adaptability. It shouldn't have included bullying, but hey, I wasn't the poster child for popularity, so I guess it was a given. The truth is, most of those who tried to hurt me during that time were usually the ones followed by loss and regret. Those departed with more to say, more to give to those they had loved and regretting not imparting the lessons they should have to them. I could see it on their faces when I'd chance a quick glance in their direction as those they had chosen to follow tormented others around them. It's a true statement, if not a bit cliché, but it holds, hurt people really do hurt people. I had found in my life, I was surrounded by a lot of hurt people.

What I didn't expect in the midst of wrestling with puberty and the assignment of social classes for the next couple of years was the increase in the things I could see and do. We had been living in that small town for a while. My isolation away from swarms of people kept me from having to deal with too much all at once, but we now lived in a much larger city, and people were everywhere. I couldn't avoid them if I tried, and I recall a few times gasping in the car when I thought my mom or dad was going to hit someone in the middle of the road, only to realize they were well past injury status. This was the true awakening of understanding the depths of my abilities. Look, it's one thing to be a kid and deal with ghosts working their way in and out of your life; it's another to understand that there was so much more you were capable of seeing.

That revelation with my elementary school teacher and what was now her own toddler running about her house was nothing compared to the emotions and flashes that would slam into me when I touched certain people. It was almost as if I had front row seats to parts of their lives that they kept locked away or needed the most help with, and that only led to the compulsion to do just that. I'd find myself forced to tell someone a random statement that barely made a lick of sense to me, but the look that would come over their face only solidified that it was exactly what they needed to hear.

So, here I was, just a gangling preteen walking through the world, a lightning rod of information for the right people at the right time. It was absolutely annoying. Had I been the least bit shy, it might have killed me. Luckily, having always been the new kid, I didn't mind talking to people I didn't know. What I did mind was not being able to be a normal twelve or thirteen-year-old kid hanging out with my friends. You can't explain that kind of weirdness away to your peers at that age; you're just marked as a little bit strange by them all. I guess it could have been worse. At least I had a friend or two who took the time to notice I was weird and still hung out with me anyway.

Of course, I couldn't get too comfortable, there was one more move around the corner for me, and it would be the last one for a long while. I remember it perfectly. My last day of eighth grade at that school was Valentine's Day. Long gone were the days of class parties. This wasn't elementary school any longer; we were too mature for those things. But me moving away was the added excuse one of my smaller classes needed to bring in cookies and whatever other sweets they could sneak in there. The party wasn't really a going-away celebration for me; over half the kids in there hadn't said more than a handful of words to me ever, but it was nice, nonetheless. Cookies are always an added bonus, no matter what the excuse for them might be. I was hoping it was the end of feeling so overwhelmed by the lost people around me and what seemed like an endless stream of connections that needed to be made. I was desperate for a moment of respite, a minute to breathe without needing to do anything for someone else.

You're selfish at that age, and the world is created and ends in your presence on a daily basis, and you feel as if you have zero control over any of it. Nothing is more frustrating to me than not being in control, but at thirteen, it's a lesson you're forced to learn nearly every hour of every day, and I hated it.

I don't know how but Friday, I was in one school, we drove a few hours down the road and started unpacking before dinner, and by Monday morning, I was the new kid all over again. I was so used to it at this point it was as if it had become my vocation, my job to force other kids my age to accept someone new into the fold or to hone their rejection skills into a fine point. All the same questions, all the same kids, and I handed out new books and instructions with a half dozen teachers, and I'd forget their names by the time I hopped on the bus. That's always the fun part, that first bus ride home. I'd lived in so many houses, I could barely remember which one I now belonged to that first week. I would figure it out one way or another.

Let me be honest, the absolute worst part of your first day in a new school, especially in middle school, is that first lunch. You've been captive in your new holding pen for only a few hours, which is not nearly enough time to assess the full hierarchical landscape of the preteen society, and one wrong step can easily lead to public chastisement and embarrassment or a lifetime of forever friendships. That's a lot to carry on one of those plastic lunch trays your first day trapped with the locals.

None of that mattered today. There I was, carrying my lunch into the courtyard, searching for any empty spot that looked safe enough for me to navigate there on my own and pull the whole "wait and see" move and enjoy my lunch when I heard over my shoulder.

"Hey, you're new. You can sit here if you want."

Turning around, she was definitely talking to me. Scooting over to prove there was an ample amount of room next to her under the tree. She looked up again, smiled, and said, "I'm Jess."

Smiling back, I couldn't help but laugh; this was a first. I hadn't expected to meet my best friend that day, but some of the best things in life are the unexpected. Setting my food down and sinking onto the ground next to her, in an instant, too much fun and too much trouble were set into motion.

"I'm Jen."

The next thing out of her mouth made me laugh so hard I nearly cried.

"So, did you hear about the ghost that haunts the school yet?"

TWENTY-ONE

New Friends

As a matter of fact, I had not heard about the infamous ghost that apparently haunted the school up to that point, but I was about to have front row seats to the entire story. Here's what I was told by almost every kid who had ever attended that campus. This ghost was a legend.

Years ago, because they always start years ago, it was homecoming night, and a young girl had been at the dance with her date. She was crowned as one of the royal court but not the queen; that story has already been written. Anyway. Her date didn't care either way and had decided to leave amidst all the celebration. The girl having fun with her friends after the crowning didn't notice he was gone for a while. She started to look for him at the dance and couldn't find him anywhere. It's said that she stood outside waiting, hoping he would come back and get her, but instead was picked up by some stranger that took her for her last ride, never to be seen again. Apparently, you can still drive by late at night past the front of the school and see her waiting for her date with her head hung low in sadness.

God, I love a good ghost story. Of course, I've got a few of my own, but not like this urban legend, where you see the ghost out of the corner of your eye when the moon is full kind of story. I had seen a few ghosts roaming the halls that morning, but none of them were wearing a crown so far. If I had to guess, it was a story made up at a sleepover by someone's older brother or sister meant to scare the crap out of the room full of kids, and from what I could tell, it must have worked. It definitely stuck, and everyone had heard of her. Famous or infamous as she may have been, I didn't think she stuck around to foster her reputation.

It was great to listen to Jess tell it. To say we were fast friends doesn't do it justice. It was almost as if we had known each other our whole lives but only just had the opportunity to meet in person. I think I was staying at her house by the end of that first weekend. We became inseparable, much to my parent's disdain at some point later on when just about everything we did led to some kind of trouble, lots of trouble.

She and I told each other everything. This means she was the only person that wasn't family or dead that knew my secrets. We all need one, a partner in crime that knows what you're going through, that can see your struggle. Jess was mine. That summer, we considered all kinds of ghost stories. We spent a lot of time researching them in the library, pre-internet remember, and thought about all of those ways to call on certain ghosts and to tempt fate. I'm sure you've heard of them, light as a feather, stiff as a board, which I've never seen work, Bloody Mary,

Ouija boards, you know, the typical scare the shit out of kids topics. We didn't try any, but that first one that summer and that was at some sleepover with a gaggle of giggling girls freezing bras and dipping sleeping hands into warm water kind of night.

There was a group of us that tended to hang out most weekends or outings, but it never failed; it was always Jess and me. I don't remember the nightmares grabbing for me too much during that time, but I'm sure they were there. What I do remember is Jess always asking if I could see any ghosts around wherever we were. It's hard to say yes without them hearing me, and we had to have a discussion as to how much I tried to keep it quiet. I wanted to have fun, not listen to a bunch of dead people all summer. We came to an agreement, and there were a few hand signals we made up for me to let her know I could see one without actually saying, "oh hey, there's a ghost over there, by the way." It helped to keep my interaction down, but the entertainment of it all still there for her. It was our own secret code, and we'd laugh every time we used it. She never once questioned that I might be lying or making it all up either. She took me at my word from that first moment we met, and I can't recall ever misleading her or lying once during our entire relationship. I'm not sure I could.

As we entered high school, hallways became more crowded, and I was waylaid by random messages and visions at nearly every turn. High school is hard enough but add in teenage secrets smacking me in the face, and I almost lost it a few times. All of us teetering between adolescence and adulthood, searching for the type of person we think we are or that we want to be. Every one of us exploring new boundaries and relationships, and I was stuck seeing way too many of them. I did not need to know what everyone was hiding or thinking. Much less did I need to add to my weirdness and tell some of them these random messages they needed to hear to move on from whatever it was they were struggling with. It was absolute hell. High school became my nightmare. Every day another secret, every other day another message. I had enough of my own problems to deal with to add all of theirs onto me too.

It made me angry most days, and had it not been for Jess, I may have crawled into myself and disappeared. Our group of friends keeping me a little closer to sanity than I would have been without them. That's probably everyone's story when it comes to their high school experience. Mine was just muddled with too many extra thoughts and secrets that never really belonged to me. I did learn one lesson rather quickly my freshman year, other people's secrets are their own, and it was never my story to tell. I know so many things about so many people that have never spoken them into existence, but their secrets are theirs and not mine.

I tried hard to avoid people. Hiding in the bathroom between classes running down the almost empty hallways and slipping into class just before the bell. More often than not, I was late and add up all those tardies, and I started to spend a lot of time in detention. Of course, we were chained at the hip, so if I had detention, Jess found a way to meet me there. Like I said, we were too much fun and too much trouble all at once. By our sophomore year, we were infamous. I had spent more time in detention than I had in class most weeks, and it was worth it.

The best thing about our sophomore year, at a certain point, we were able to drive. Freedom at that age is dangerous. You feel invincible, and you behave as if you are as well. You'd think I'd know better, so many young people I'd seen walking around lost from one stupid reason or another. I suppose it doesn't matter what all you've been through when you're fifteen and sixteen or how mature you are from the way life has smacked you around. You're still a damn idiot most of the time. I was no exception. It was as if the moment I was handed a driver's license and a set of car keys, my brain no longer functioned at its previous capacity. I had never been more reckless in my life than those first few months behind the wheel, and heaven help me if Jess was driving. I about stomped a hole into the floorboard of her mom's minivan more times than I can count, and I'm pretty sure if you pull up the rug, there's a dent in the shape of my foot.

Having gained the ability to move about the world on our own just added to our list of trouble that we found ourselves into on a weekly basis. Instead of being late for class, we'd manage to forget to go at all. There were many such adventures, and we explored a lot of dark corners in our town. How we managed to still have access to fresh air at times is beyond me, but somehow, we were caught less than we should have been and in danger more than we could have possibly known. I live with the knowledge that I've earned every hour of my life, but there were many that I know were almost stolen when I wasn't guarding them properly. It only took one ride into the woods to remind me of just what could happen and exactly what was waiting deep inside some of those dark corners.

TWENTY-TWO

Into the Woods

It was late, and I'm sure we were out well past our curfew, which means we were likely staying at Jess's house. Her parents never really paid too much attention to the time, at least not most of the time. We had driven to the other side of town and found ourselves playing pool with a couple of guys we kind of knew from school that were just a bit older than we were. The plan was to finish up the game and take a drive into the dark to inhale some of the foliage, so to speak. It's a good thing I had the ability to tell when someone was a "good" person or not. Can you imagine two sixteen-year-old girls jumping into the car of some eighteen or nineteen-year-old guy that we barely even knew his name? These are the situations that Liam Neeson movies are based on or one of those after-school specials we've all sat and watched.

Tucked away in the tiny backseat of his hatchback, whatever it was, we drove off into the park. I don't remember the name of the park, which isn't surprising; we've already established how epic my memory is. What I can tell you is it was the only time I've ever been to it, and I have no plans to ever return again. We pulled up to one of the little cabins that littered the park, not sure if it was one you could rent out and camp in or one used by maintenance, but there wasn't a light on one. In fact, the entire area was pitch black. The headlights of his car shining onto the picnic table there off to the side, and we three slid out of our seats to find a new one there on those wooden benches. It really was one of those "I could kill you here" types of places. Every single red flag should have been waving for both Jess and me, but nope, invincible.

I think we were at the table for all of five minutes when I felt an all too familiar feeling. Not the telltale sign of a ghost or that I was getting anything from this guy we were sitting alone in the woods with either. No, this was a feeling I hadn't had in a very long time except in my dreams. The feeling of walking up to that tree in my grandparent's front yard all those years ago or that bedroom in that house of horrors I lived in, that was the sensation creeping up all around us. The two of them oblivious as every hair on my body stood at attention. As if they were antenna picking up the signal of a broadcast of fear and pain, and I was tuned into it and nothing else.

I was surrounded by the sounds of their conversation and not hearing a single word of it. I could feel the darkness creeping in closer, the light from the headlights not as bright as they were when we first arrived and dimming more with every passing moment. I could feel my heart starting to pound in my chest, and the fear of what I knew was out there starting to take over my every thought.

I had pushed past it so many times, and here I was going to lose to it in the middle of some park I never knew the name of with some guy in a shitty hatchback car with crappy weed. This was not how I was going to let it win, not tonight, and definitely not like this.

"We have to go."

It's all I said, and I looked at Jess directly without another word. There was no mistaking my need to get the hell out of there, and she didn't for a second try to argue it with me either. She looked over at the guy who drove us into this trap so willingly, and I suspected unknowingly and repeated my words. Now he tried to argue it with her, but you know what works? Tell a guy just old enough to get in trouble getting caught alone in the woods with a couple of underage girls that you're going to start screaming, and they manage to find it in their best interest to pack up and move along back into a public forum.

I needed out of there, and I needed out of there right now. My breathing was only getting faster as the darkness moved in closer around the table. My hands shaking at the thought that we might not make it back into the car without being brushed by the edges of what had surrounded us. That wail I had filed away deep into a dark closet in the back of my mind from the connection made to it when my grandmother touched that tree let loose and ripped through me, grabbing hold of the edges of my sanity trying to pull me into the abyss. The cold locked away in that room, inching closer with every second we sat there. I was frozen. That fight or flight reaction again leading to my feet cemented to the ground, unable to move in any direction. Had Jess not touched my arm as she stood up, I might still be sitting at that picnic table now, a hollowed-out version of myself or what was left of me once I had been consumed by the nightmare that haunted me with and without my eyes closed.

I could barely feel my feet underneath me as I stumbled back to the car, and Jess half dragged me with her. Climbing into the back of the car, I couldn't catch my breath. I needed us to move. I needed to be out of there. My voice caught in the back of my throat in a silent scream wanting to yell, "run" at the top of my lungs. I didn't know what it could do to me or to any of us, for that matter. What I knew was I didn't want to find out.

Completely unaware of the panic building inside of me, our driver took his time and had it been appropriate to smack him in the back of the head, I would have. Jess, on the other hand, as if reading my mind, punched him in the arm and told him to hurry his ass up. I think the moment he finally looked into the rearview mirror and saw the panic on my face, did he care to know what was going on. Instead of wasting time with some "what's wrong with you" line of questioning, I jumped forward in my seat and looked him in the eyes through the mirror and asked the only question that matter to me at that moment.

"Why did you take us there? Why did you take us to that spot? Why?"

TWENTY-THREE

The Story

This was not the drive he had been expecting to have, and looking back at me, his eyes narrowed in confusion. Not sure how to wrestle my interrogation, he slowly backed out of the place we had parked and finally moved forward and towards the exit. How he managed to drive with his eyes locked on mine, I'll never know, but he didn't break from the stare until we reached the gate. He didn't look away until he'd pulled onto the road and out of the park. Never once saying a word or looking at either of us, it was as if he planned to ignore my questions and just take us back to our car. That may have been his plan, but it sure as hell wasn't mine.

Now that we were out of the wooded area and moving at a faster speed, my breathing started to normalize, as did my heart, and the fear of the moment was left back at that picnic table for now. I needed to know why he had brought us there. Had he been pulled to that place by the darkness without knowing it, or was it just some strange coincidence that led us to that spot and into the reaches of the one thing I'd been keeping my distance from for years? Either way, I needed to know, and I didn't believe in coincidences.

There was only about a ten-minute drive between that gate and the waiting minivan, and I hoped it was enough time to gather some answers as to what had just happened. Jess turned back to look at me with a bit of fear behind her eyes, not at our near miss; she had no idea that had even happened. She was afraid for me. I'd never been more afraid around her, and she was terrified as to what it might have meant. I gave her the watered-down version of those experiences and nightmares before. The fun for her was knowing that there were ghosts all around, not this unknown stalking me. It didn't matter what I had told her before; she knew that if I had been scared, there was reason to really be scared.

"Well, are you going to answer me or not? Why did you take us there? Why that spot?"

He gave me an irritated look in the mirror and shot back his response.

"I go there all the time. I live around the damn corner. Why the hell did you two get all freaked out all of a sudden. What's the matter, little girls scared of the dark?"

I gave him that "you are just stupid" look, but Jess hauled off and punched him in the arm again, punctuated with the following declaration.

"The hell I'm scared of the dark, you idiot."

"Hey, you crazy bitches! What the hell is going on with you two? I thought we were just going out there to smoke a little and then come back and play some more pool. Instead, the two of you went all psycho and shit."

He was going to grow up to understand and listen to people; that much was clear, and I couldn't stop my eyes rolling in response. If he only knew what was out there, he'd be thanking me for getting us out of there when I did.

"Believe what you want, but there was something out there. Something wasn't right, and I think you know it too."

His head whipped back in my direction as his eyes narrowed in accusation. There was something behind that thought, and he knew I could see it. I didn't care that it was his secret. I wasn't going to get out of his car until I knew why he went out there. He was hiding something, and I couldn't see it yet, but he wasn't going to be able to hide it from me for long. This is one of those times my gifts would have come in handy. Instead, I was stuck arguing with a man child about what's hiding in the woods. It was turning into the worst scavenger hunt and game of hide and go seek ever. I could see more questions on their way when all I really wanted was some answers.

"What do you mean there was something out there?"

That's it, I was done. I could not sit there with all of this back-and-forth questioning any longer. It was time to figure this out. I leaned forward, putting my hand on his shoulder, hoping that the physical connection would help me in some way to see what he was hiding, and asked again.

"Why that spot?"

He jumped in his seat at my touch, and the car swerved a bit to the left as if not only him, but the car was trying to get away from me and the question. I couldn't see it all, but I could sense the loss and the pain that lived in that place for him. There was a reason he went there, he had a genuine connection to that space, and it was hard for him to admit.

The question was going to continue to hang out there for eternity if I didn't push him along. To Jess's credit, she sat quietly, keeping an eye on the road in case she needed to grab the wheel. She may have had a thousand questions she wanted answered at that moment, but she was more disciplined than I might have been and kept them to herself for the time being.

"There's pain there. I can feel it. Why do you go there? I need you to tell me, please."

Since asking directly wasn't working, maybe a little finesse would help, and well, please is the magic word, right? He just stared back at me, but now there was a softness around the edges of his eyes. I could see the tears threatening to break the surface, ready to find their escape. It was too late now. No matter how much he wanted to hold it all back, his lips began to betray him.

"My brother died out there. Murdered, actually, but why do you care? And what the hell do you mean you can feel it?"

Backtracking my statement, I stumble a little bit over it.

"I meant I could see it. You looked sad out there. It didn't feel right."

He nodded his head as if that made perfect sense, but I was still reeling at the realization that someone had been murdered out there. At least now I knew why he was drawn to that place, and I was willing to bet that the darkness lurking out there held some responsibility in his brother's death as well. I was going to ask what happened, but my part in this wasn't necessary any longer. He began recounting the entire story. Every painful memory of those events spilled out of him, and somehow, I knew this would no longer hold him here later on, and he would find a way to rest when it was his time.

I'm not sure if it was the first time I had helped the living find their way to peace before they were haunted and tethered here, but it's the first time I recognized it. Something about my hand grounding the pain gave him the freedom to release it all. Jess and I listened to every word and bore witness to every tear. I'm not sure when we pulled into the parking lot or how long we had been sitting there when he was done, but each moment accounted for a lifetime of pain removed from his shoulders.

His brother's death, that was another story altogether. He had been out there with friends, behaving in about the same way the three of us had planned on enjoying our night. Five guys having fun in the woods, the headlights of the car a spotlight illuminating the life and times of these teenage boys. It's a secluded park, and you could be as loud as you wanted, and they were whooping and hollering in kind, poking fun at each other and having a great time. It all sounds harmless, and in reality, it should have been. Most people don't find their way to places like that unless they're set to have a good time.

Not one of them had known the danger they were in sitting there. How they were surrounded by something so full of darkness and pain, something waiting for any opportunity to unleash itself upon this world. It's the only explanation as to what happened next, and the man that walked up to these boys probably still doesn't realize how he was only a pawn in this game played by evil.

He had been one of the caretakers there of the park and had been called by a supervisor letting him know that there had been a report of a group of teenagers getting a little too rowdy near one of the buildings. They sent him out there to break it up and ensure that there wasn't any damage to any of the property. All he would have had to do was tell them it was time to pack it up and move on, but that's not what happened. He never said a word, not one word.

The boys never even saw him coming until it was too late. He had walked up behind his brother first and took a swing at his head with a baseball bat as if it were opening day. His brother was dead before he hit the ground, and the other boys launched quickly into their flight mode, jumping into their car, and flying out of the park. When the police arrived a little while later, the boy laid there on the ground, gone, and the caretaker sat in the middle of the picnic table with the bat in his lap. His mood swinging between tears of disbelief and a silent stare. He didn't speak a single word until they pulled out of the park, and only then did he ask what had happened.

He's serving a life sentence now for something only his body participated in, and I'm sure he spends every day trying to remember what really happened that night. If he had truly known what it was, he would only be trying to forget.

I took my hand from his arm, watched as he pulled in a deep breath, and finally released it all. I motioned for Jess to open the door, and as we climbed out of the car, he looked over to me and smiled.

Now we could go.

TWENTY-FOUR

Are you okay?

I debated a few times on whether or not I should go back out there to see if his brother was hanging around or at peace, but I couldn't bring myself to do it. I couldn't chance being caught up in it all or trapped there, and Jess wasn't about to let me either. She spent the better part of the next few days trying to bring me back to a fun and somewhat normal place. It was evident that night had shaken something from me, and I needed to be pulled back out of it. Of course, the nightmares started back in full force, and I spent that first week half asleep during the day because I had done nothing but run from what was trying to pull me into oblivion every night. After a while, it all settled back down, and I was back to feeling invincible. Learning my way through life and into adulthood was littered with bad decisions, and too many of them I should have avoided.

I managed to survive my bouts of stupidity and found my way into my junior year. Still the same,

Jess and I rounding every turn in trouble, but we did get better at hiding it. Our lives only revolving around school and parties. I can't remember a lot of things I was supposed to be learning in class, but I had no issue remembering where each hidden party was for that weekend. At a certain point, we quit caring, and at our friend, Jo's house, was the perfect place to go crazy. Her parents were always out of town and working nights, and she lived in a neighborhood full of people who couldn't care less what we were all up to as long as we kept it somewhat contained. Having to only deal with the onslaught of flashing lights on that rare occasion, some idiot got more than a little out of hand, which only had to happen a few times before that lesson was learned.

I felt that I was living my life in those moments, just a normal kid hanging out with friends doing all the things we weren't supposed to be doing, and I could ignore the rest. I found that a drink here or there helped to dampen everything around me, and I could skate through a night, not once noticing anything out of the ordinary that others couldn't see. This isn't a sales tactic condoning that you do what I did, but the mistakes are part of my story, and even with the normalcy it helped to create, it doesn't mean it was the right choice either.

It was at one such party that I went too far, drank a little too much like you do, and found myself blind to the world I had come to know as normal, and it was just my friends and me having a great time. Of course, there were always a few people there I didn't know. Most people didn't know each other for that matter. It's the way of the high school party, strangers amongst friends. However, that night was the first night I can remember being flung back into my purpose in an instant. The world was fuzzy, giggles and slurred speech my new status, and I expected to find a dark corner to curl up in sooner rather than later to start to sleep it off. I was going to regret the drink I was currently holding in the morning, but hey, I was invincible.

Working my way down the hall, I brushed up against someone I'd never seen before, and everything flipped. I was sober in an instant, and regardless of where I had thought I was going, I felt drawn to her and compelled to sit with her. I couldn't explain it, and as I set my cup on the side table in the living room, I fell onto the couch and into her presence. Someone had something to say to her, or there was something she needed to know, and I quickly introduced myself before I started looking like some crazy girl just staring at her. We chatted for a few minutes about nothing and everything all at once. There was a reason I'd never seen her before; she was only in town for the week visiting a cousin who we did go to school with and was over in another corner here at the party chatting up some other girl.

The only real problem sitting there talking with her was I knew her secret. I knew exactly why she was visiting, and I knew she wanted nothing more than to never go back. Sadly, I also understood why. It's not a topic you toss around at some booze-filled high school party, either. She was hurting and clawing out her insides, screaming for help without ever saying a word. I remember her name too, but her secrets are not mine to tell, and I'll keep that tidbit of information to myself. That way, I could be talking about anyone.

We talked for hours that night, and at one point, late into the morning hours, I asked her, "Are you okay?" Memories of Bobby and me hiding in my closet flew through my mind. I knew if she didn't find a way to get it out, she too would be hugging her knees in pain after finding her own way to leave pieces of herself scattered everywhere. I didn't want that for her, and I think that thought of Bobby was the reason I knew this was a turning point moment. A location in a person's life where they can choose their direction, and she was leaning towards a full stop instead of continuing down any other path available to her.

She looked at me quizzically when I asked, we had just been laughing moments earlier, and she was lost as to why I might inquire about her wellbeing. Wasn't it obvious to me that she had her happy mask on tonight? That was the problem, I could see behind the mask, and there was nothing happy back there. I had tried to ignore it, tried to just have a good time and sip on my drink there on the table, but no matter how much more I tried to drink, it had zero effect on me. I might as well have been drinking water, and I one point, that was what I decided to do. It made no sense to keep trying something I knew wasn't going to work on making me forget why I was sitting there in the first place. So, I asked again.

"Are you okay?"

What started off as her nodding her head slowly turned into her shaking it and with it the tears that had been trapped behind her eyes. There were no words, only the sadness pulling at every corner of her face now. I took her hand and pulled her away into a quiet room where for several more hours, she confessed the secret of the abuse she'd been living through and trying to survive. Young girls, or boys for that matter, shouldn't have to tell that kind of story, and they shouldn't have to hold ownership of the pain caused to them by those who are supposed to love them. A lesson I knew all too well, but her pain, that was one I couldn't begin to understand. Such a travesty pushed upon her and for way too long. No one knew, not one other person other than the two of us there behind the closed door in that quiet room. Of course, the abuser knew. They sat thinking they had all the control now after so many years of slipping into her room at night or taking advantage of her while no one else was around. Do you know what happens when someone who has lived through terror finds their voice? It may start off small or even just a whisper, but the second it's been found, the chains of control are broken, and freedom is found, and there is no room for silence.

That's what was uncovered there in that room, and as the sun started to peek through the window, as dawn found its way to light the world once more, she had found a way to live in it for the first time all over again.

TWENTY-FIVE

Just a Game

I attended several such parties at Jo's house, the three of us usually ending up talking all night as people trickled out or passed out wherever they fell until we were sleeping in her huge bed waiting for the party to wear off. That particular weekend wasn't any different than most of the ones before or after it, for that matter. This night when I walked through the door, something was off, something wasn't right, and it was not the normal fun-loving feeling I had been used to stepping into when I was at her house. I didn't know what it was, and it was going to be hours before I found out. Sitting there amongst everyone with that uneasiness scratching at the back of my mind, teasing my instincts into a heightened sense of alert. It's a difficult way to feel when you're trying to have good time.

That was always my goal. I spent the rest of the week surround by responsibility, whether that meant school, chores or what had quickly become an irritation in my life. The weekends were for forgetting about it all and just being a dumb kid without a care in the world. I had perfected those moments. Once I made the mistake of making eye contact with a ghost trailing behind a kid I didn't know and spent well over half the night listening to them ramble on about one regret or another. I had tired of it all, and I didn't want to have to deal with it anymore. If I could have figured out a way to turn it off or make it go away forever, during those few years, I would have signed my name on the dotted line for a glimpse of ordinary. Instead, they only grew stronger, and my irritation grew deeper. If you think most teenagers are moody, you should hang out around one that is dealing not only with the real world but the dead as well. It started to feel a lot like I was being followed by three annoying ankle-biters again at every turn. Only this time, I couldn't yell at them to go away and leave me alone. It was just another part of my life where I found myself trapped by circumstance.

That night went as most did, but it was cold out, and people found their way home sooner than they might have on a typical night. It was going to be one of those toss on our pajamas and see what shakes loose from the emotional tree kind of parties for our trio. The three of us back in Jo's room lounging in one fashion or another on that monstrous bed of hers. I don't know how she managed this giant bed, but we could have fit another five people on there and still had room to spread out. It nearly took up the entire room.

Giggles and gossip ensued, and we were performing our usual routine for a night like this one and finding our own laid-back fun. In mid-sentence, Jo stopped, that look of, "oh yeah, I almost forgot," plastered to her face as she jumped off the bed and ran into the other room. Walking back in with a long thin box in hand, I sighed at the realization that she had produced yet another board game for us to trudge through. I hate board games. They might as well be called bored games as far as I'm concerned. What an absolute waste of time and focus when we could have just been enjoying the conversation. The smirk on her face was one that told me she thought she had found the right one this time, and she giggled as both Jess, and I let out an audible groan in protest.

"No, really, I've got it this time, guys. Look."

She tossed the box onto the bed between us, and I instantly recoiled. No. No, no, no, no. I can't touch that thing. I don't want to touch that thing. It was not a game, at least not to me it wasn't. To other kids my age, it was the new trend, the fun "game" to play. Unlike light as a feather, stiff as a board, this one was real. It had consequences, especially for someone like me. I pushed all the way back on the bed and pressed myself against the wall as if it were going to bite me, and the two of them just giggled, opening up the box and getting it set up. Neither of them noticing or paying any attention to my trepidation on the matter. Their comments of excitement and curiosity increasingly made me realize that I would not be able to get out of this, and I needed to just take a deep breath and remind myself that it would all be alright. Deep down, I knew it was not all going to be alright.

The lid of the box lay casually next to my foot, and I spent a good minute focused on the disclaimer on the box, "2 or more players." The whole thing was marketed as a game you sat to play, but it didn't feel like a game to me. Of course, she had to get the one with a horned devil in the middle. Let's just add to the sinisterness of it all, and I'll just sit here petrified by what everyone pushed off as just a toy. When it was set up there in the middle of us, the board and the planchette with its clear crystal snapped into place to magnify each letter as it was chosen, with the word Ouija posted there at the top, I fought every instinct to run. I took one last deep breath, looked at the two of them in turn, and they were beside themselves with excitement. Jo picking up the instructions to skim them quickly before they both leaned over to put the tips of their fingers in place, and I left sitting there trying to find a way out of it all.

Do you know what the instructions boil down to? Lightly place your fingertips onto the planchette, ask the board a question, and wait to see what it answers. The problem is, once one of these things are pulled out of the box, any ghost within a mile is drawn towards it, and I figured it was about to get really crowded on this big bed. Now, that's the harmless side of it. I mean harmless to all the people who can't see them. I was going to be staring at this one daisy on Jo's comforter for the foreseeable future until the room was cleared again. Unfortunately, that was not going to happen any time soon. I could feel them already being drawn to the board, and I groaned again at what was happening. Let's be clear, this "game" doesn't just call the happy-go-lucky bunch of dead in the area, it calls to them all, and I knew the odds of their not being something dark and foreboding was slim to none. That was what kept me from touching the thing. I'd only be a lightning rod for those lost, angry souls pulled towards me like a slingshot. I couldn't be any part of that, and

I pushed deeper into the wall. I would've melt into it if I could, but I hadn't perfected that particular superpower yet, but boy, I sure wish I had.

Just as I was about to volunteer to keep up with the responses, Jo grabbed my arm and pulled me forward with just enough force to knock me off balance with my hands landing directly onto the board. The planchette between my palms and held in place by my forefingers. In an instant, everything went black. I couldn't see anything but the darkness surrounding me, and I screamed out in response. Of course, they interpreted that to mean I had just been taken by surprise, and they laughed at my perceived skittishness. The truth was that I had found that place past petrified. I had been pulled inside with that darkness now, and it was no longer going to stalk me. It was now going to try and consume me.

I pulled back as if it had bitten me and curled up around myself. Frozen again. Another moment I wish I had the ability to choose which response showed up in these instances. Instead, here I was, locked in place by a damn board. Jess looked over at me differently now and realized it was not me overreacting, I had more going on than she and Jo could see, and she knew it. Leaning over, she touched my knee, asking if I was alright, and I jumped back from the connection. I needed a moment to shake it all off, and that was about all I was going to be allowed as the room was starting to fill with those trying to take control and get out their message.

I took in a deep breath and held it for a moment, letting the air push against my lungs and force me to focus on something else. Your body tries to take over, reminding you that you need to exhale, that you need to take in another breath. You're pushed into the realization that you cannot survive on that one gulp of air forever, your lungs fighting to pull in more, to serve their purpose, and just breathe. I needed to just breathe. I couldn't change where I was now, and even if I did try to leave, it wouldn't matter; they'd all follow me. I looked up at Jess and nodded that I was alright. I could do this no matter how hard I knew it was going to be. I kept a close eye on the people who had filtered into the bedroom, and the three of them stood there waiting to try their hand at communicating with anyone willing to listen.

I looked up and directly at one of the women standing there, the three of them acknowledging that I could see them, and their souls lit up for a brief second. I took in one more deep breath, unfolded myself as I looked over at my friends, and said, "Alright, let's see what these spirits have to say."

Jo clapped in excitement, and I sat back and watched as the two of them argued over what questions to ask first. I looked back up at the first woman, patted the bed beside me, and waited for her story. By the end of the night, I had heard them all, but that's not to say that board wasn't still haunting me. They'd ask a few questions, get bored with it for a bit, grab another drink until they'd set it up to play with it once more. I started to think that maybe I had freaked out a little more than I should have, but as the last ghost wrapped up his list of regrets and slipped away, they laid their hands on it for one final try. Before they could argue over the next question, Jo burst forth with one neither of us had expected, and it flung me straight into the freak-out carnival I had been avoiding all night.

"Are you the darkness?"

Jess and I whipped our heads in her direction, and I swear my jaw bounce off the bed a few times. Before I could ask her what she said or why she asked such a question, the pointer flew to "yes," neither Jo nor Jess actually touching it. They pulled their hands back from the board and looked from face to face. This was not what either of them had expected.

"Wh-why would you ask that?"

She shook off what looked like a haze she'd been locked in for a second and couldn't remember even asking.

"Ask what? I didn't ask anything."

Jess and I stared hard at each other and back at Jo. Surely, she was messing with us. We had both just heard her ask.

"Yes, you did. You just asked that board a question. We both heard you."

Before she could deny it again, the pointer moved itself to the word, "no." Now all three of us jumped back from the board, not knowing exactly what to do. Jess shouted out exactly what we were all thinking.

"What the hell?!"

Still, without any of us touching the board, the planchette moved on its own, stopping at each letter long enough for us to catch it. D - A - R - K. Three times, it slid across the board on its own, and three times it spelled exactly the same thing. This time we all screamed. Jo grabbed the board and flung it, pointer, and all into the farthest corner from us, with it crashing hard into the wall. We sat there for a moment in disbelief, and I stared over at the broken board, hoping that was the end of it. I knew deep down it wasn't.

"Nope. That's enough of that shit, and I sure as

hell can't sleep now. Let's go watch some stupid movie somewhere else. Like, now."

Jo jumped off the bed before she'd even finished talking and was out the door without looking back once. Jess looked over at the corner and then back at me.

"You okay?"

I thought about it for a minute and nodded my head in response. I honestly wasn't sure, but I was glad to be away from that thing. We slid off the bed and headed towards the sound of the television coming to life in the living room. I'm don't recall what movie Jo landed on, nor do I really remember watching any of it. I was well past exhausted, and I think I was out before the title screen ever popped up. I sure we all passed out just before the sun came up, and we slept there on the couch and floor for the better part of the next day. It was when we woke up and filed back into Jo's room to grab some fresh clothes and our toothbrushes that we noticed the board was gone. For a second, we thought maybe Jo's mom had come home and found the broken board in the corner and threw it away, but she wasn't expected back in town until tomorrow.

We looked from one face to the other and started searching. The damn thing had to be here somewhere, but it wasn't. We looked everywhere, and it wasn't until Jess plopped herself down onto the bed and looked up that she screamed. Following her gaze toward the ceiling, Jo and I added our voices to the roar of panic. There pieced together on the ceiling was the board, the planchette pointing directly at the devil in the center. Jess flew up from the bed, and we stood there frozen as the board fell from the ceiling, landing in pieces on the bed where she had just been. That was it, no more, I couldn't take anymore. I grabbed the board and the pointer and ran down the hallway and out the back door. Opening the grill lid so quickly, I nearly knocked the entire thing over, but I managed to toss the pieces of our nightmare into it as Jess grabbed the lighter fluid from the concrete table beside it. Stepping back, a stream of accelerant arched onto this "game" inside, and before the last drop could land, Jo flung in a lit match. The entire board lit up like a fireworks display. We collectively held our breath. Not one of us moved an inch until all that was left was ash. I'm not sure we blinked as it all burned, and when the final flame died down, then, and only then did we feel free enough to breathe again.

TWENTY-SIX

Sleep

Everything was different after that night. We didn't speak of it again either, but each time we looked into the face of the other, we relived it minute by minute. None of us had ever been more scared in our lives, even me, with everything I had seen. It was as if we had opened a doorway. Allowing for more of the darkness to creep in and take over, and for a brief moment, I had been connected to it. I was starting to see it for what it was. Fragments placed here and there, taking over unassuming individuals that found themselves close enough to the pain and fear. We were all susceptible to its drawl; not everyone was aware of it, though. Some people were consumed by it for years, calling to it and carrying it around like a badge of honor. Wrapped within the darkness like a fuzzy blanket keeping out all that was good and right that they could grasp hold of for salvation. Instead, living within it willingly.

What it was capable of scared me. What it was, what I was realizing is it was riddled with sadness and loneliness. I didn't know what to do about it anymore, and I felt surrounded at every turn. Nights were the worst. I'd lay in bed trying to quiet my mind when something would take over and slowly start to chant a call for it to come closer. Inviting it to share space and time with me. I could hear it scratching at the window, see it in the bathroom mirror, or the reflection of anything with a shiny enough surface. I was now too close, and I didn't know how to put that space between us again.

I would be petrified by the time my body would give out on me, and I'd fall asleep from sheer exhaustion. The end of my junior year was the hardest one I've ever crawled my way through. The dark circles under my eyes only growing deeper with each day, and I tried everything to find a way to forget. There were many nights I found myself sneaking into my parent's room and sliding under the edges of their bed, finally finding sleep to the sounds of their breathing and my dad's snoring. Something about being close to them made me feel safe. I think I was safer there, just as I had been curled up in the hallway of that house when I was little. My mother's protection was stronger than either of us knew, and those few nights I was able to climb into their presence, I slept. It was the only time I did rest for those first four or five months before the summer.

I lived on a razor's edge every day and found myself dozing off in class and back in detention quite a bit because of it. Jess and Jo had similar issues. They weren't being haunted by the darkness. They had found themselves unable to wipe away the memory of the fear that had taken over that night. You can't slip off that feeling of panic as easily as you think you can. Especially when you can't explain exactly what happened or why. If you can't find a purpose for something like that to exist, the lines of reality easily blur, and you're never truly sure as to what might be sneaking around you or for what reason.

There it is again, the fear of the unknown. One they didn't know they had until that night was over, but then again, that's one night that is never over. No matter how hard we tried, that one was going to replay in the back of our minds over and over again like a cult classic at a drive-in theater. I tried so hard to file that one away, it wouldn't stick. I had been touched by it, and it wasn't about to let me go, not this time. It had tasted blood, so to speak, and it only wanted more.

I cried a lot during those months, not out of sadness but fear. Have you ever been so afraid that your body can no longer fully relax? That's how I felt all day, every day. I needed to get away from it. I needed a break from the tension being pulled tight inside my body before it all snapped.

I resorted to every tactic I could imagine to find a way to sleep and escape. I'd read, watch tv, whatever I could think of until my eyelids slammed together like a car crash. I even tried prayer. That's not accurate, I begged. I'd lay there in bed and beg for it to stop, plead for just one quiet moment that wasn't surrounded by this torment, but it didn't work. None of it did. The only remedy I found was the one attached to a bottle. It wasn't unheard of that we'd all sit around getting drunk on the weekends. I've admitted it willingly so far. However, for the last three months of my junior year, I spent every weekend at the bottom of a bottle in order to sleep.

I wasn't concerned with having a good time any longer. I wanted to rest. I needed a deep sleep where a volcanic eruption couldn't shake me free from the sandman.

Of course, I took a considerable risk in the fact that I could fall so deep and still find myself entangled by the nightmare, running from the van, hiding, ducking for cover, and knowing at each turn I'd find it there. I knew the risks; I needed the reward. I wasn't careful about it either, invincible remember. We'd sneak our way into the clubs with our fake IDs, and yet, my mission would be the same. I recall one such night that I woke in the cab of a truck. I had no idea who it belonged to or how I stumbled my way into it. I assume that's exactly what happened. I had found several glasses turned upside down in my wake, and with lack of a cushy place to land, I went in search of one. I still wonder how many handles I pulled before I found one that opened or whose truck it might have been. That was a night I could have vanished during my own last ride, just like the infamous ghost haunting the entrance into the junior high, but it wasn't.

My prayers may not have been answered for peace, but something was keeping me safe. I stumbled out of the truck and back into the bar after God only knows how long I had been in there. I'm sure I managed my way through a few more drinks and slid onto one of those pleather booths and handed over my ticket to dreamland. It could have been the side of the road for all I knew, and most of the time, I couldn't tell you how I made it to whoever's house, I ended up waking up inside of the next morning either. I needed the sleep, but I needed to find a safer way of getting it too.

By the end of the school year, I couldn't recall the better part of the last half of it. The entire spring was a blur, the fog so thick and created by a lack of sleep and self-medicating. I had to have looked like I was going to fall out at any moment to my parents, and my mother made a decision for me without a word allowed in protest. When that final school bell rang to end out that year, my mother was out front waiting for me, bags packed and an adventure ahead. She no longer knew how to help me, so it was time for her own reinforcements. A half a day later, I was pouring out of the car and into the arms of my grandmother. My whole body relaxed in an instant, and I never felt more ready for a nap in my entire life. Taking my hand and pulling me into the house, I looked back once just to be sure, and that tree stood there proud and beautiful, and only a tree. Just as it should be.

TWENTY-SEVEN

The Visit

I didn't know how much I needed to be there until I was inside their house. It was as if I had been given the opportunity to step out of myself or at least out of the self I had been for the last several months. The balled-up fear and anxiety left on the other side of the door, unable to cross the threshold into this space, and all I wanted to do was sleep. I hugged my grandparents again and crawled into the bed I'd grown accustomed to years ago and fell into an oblivion of dreamless renewal. I had practically ceased to exist once my eyes were closed, nothing able to penetrate the exhaustion that had been holding me hostage for months until now.

It was the next afternoon when I finally opened my eyes again, having slept almost an entire day, and when I crawled out of bed, I could feel the calm I had so desperately needed wash over me. It was a similar feeling I had having crawled under my parent's bed to catch a night or two of sleep but magnified to the point I almost felt normal.

What did that even mean? Here I was, seventeen, living my life in and out of death, running from the darkness only to find a path into a different kind of prison, one that required me to kill off a piece of myself at every corner. I couldn't continue to slice off bits one inch at a time; it wasn't solving anything, only leaving more broken parts to figure out how to glue back together into a real person. I had become an empty shell filled with pain swirling around in a maelstrom of darkness and uncertainty. My nightmares consuming me from the inside out. One step into this house, and the storm was nearly silenced. Hours of sleep, wiping away the exhaustion, and the pieces began to reform, to find the places where they had once fit so perfectly. Stitched back together, but never exactly the way it once was. It never could be again.

That's the reality in which we live-broken over and over, glued back together only to be broken again by something or someone else. Never fully healed, the fine cracks always visible or felt as you run your fingertips over the surface of those memories. Forever changing into the person, we continue to become. It takes a special kind of person to see them or to be allowed to get close enough to map the lines out one by one. We all have them, some of us more than others, and at this point, I had a veritable spiderweb of cracks hidden just beneath the surface. Some deeper than others, some with missing pieces that never quite fit back into place or were never found and just lost along the way. Each one bringing up a different memory, its own pain. Those of us who can't bear the pain hide them or pretend they don't exist or, like me, have found ways to heal them more than they were before. Some filler to smooth them out, the depth of the crack lessened, and actual healing allowed. That's what I needed right now, some filler, healing from the terror that had taken hold of me in an instant and had yet to let go.

The plan was for me to stay for a few weeks and try to find my way back to some sense of normal while I had a break from the reality I had been living in before. My mother hugging me, and heading out the next day, I was within the sanctity of these walls, the sentries standing guard and protecting my sanity, the fragile pieces of what was left of it at the moment, needed time to heal and regroup. Pulling me back through before the void claimed me for good.

I spent the first few days becoming friends with the pillows at the head of that bed, catching up on the sleep that had eluded me repeatedly for months. After a few days of barely seeing sunlight, I finally emerged, looking and feeling like the undead rising for the first time in centuries. My grandparents enjoyed the paper and their coffee at the dining table, lifting their gaze just enough to make sure it was me and not some random intruder searching for the funny pages. I grabbed my own cup of coffee and, according to my grandfather, bastardized it with too much cream and sugar to be able to still call it coffee. In retaliation, I grabbed the comics from the pile of unread paper in front of him, one of the few things that were against the rules in his house. No one read the paper before he did. Daring a glance in his direction, I smirked and pretended not to see him glaring at me in disbelief of my blatant disregard of the rules. The only thing saving me was the giggle it pulled from my grandmother's lips. Living only to hear her happiness, I had been saved from the paper miser for the time being.

I spent the next few days in what amounted to silence. Finding the time to assess the things I'd seen and been through and trying to determine what I needed to do next. My grandparents gave me the space I needed to work through what I could on my own before offering any additional help or advice. They always allotted me the right to live within my own life before asking any of those necessary questions that push us past the boundaries we had seen and into a fuller understanding of the fact that they never really existed in the first place. They were a form of contemplative prayer for me, a way of releasing the restraints I always placed upon the world and my place within it. I was capable of anything, and they would lift me up in the successes as well as the failures. A grounding wire reminding me that we are all only what we allow ourselves to be, and we are only held back by our own fear to push forward. My belief in people came from their belief in me.

I existed in a bubble for a few weeks there with them. Regaining my strength, as if the closeness of them was somehow healing me from the inside out, and maybe it was. I spoke with my grandmother for hours on end about what all had transpired over the last year, but especially that night. I couldn't seem to shake off. There was no judgment of my actions after the fact. It was hard to tell her how far I felt I had fallen, but I figured she knew even more than I told her before I was ever chauffeured onto their driveway. Having someone I could speak so freely with about these things and not once made to feel as if I had lost my mind was wonderful. The conversations I'm required to hold within myself on a daily basis are heavy and weigh me down at times, but here, it was the same as discussing the weather or the latest book I'd read.

My grandfather had been around such things since the minute he met her all those years ago, and I genuinely believe he could sense it within her from that very first moment. There's something about him that makes people feel wrapped in calmness when he's nearby. Maybe that's his superpower, who knows, but when I was in his presence, it was like I was surrounded by white noise or ocean waves washing over me, removing anything that didn't strengthen me. After coffee and the paper during those weeks, I'd follow him into the garage like a little puppy dog devoted to the one they love so dearly. I'd sit and watch him work, the smell of sawdust and the sounds of the machines creating a separate world that only existed within those walls. The quiet moments as he glued and pieced things together to ensure there was a stronger hold than just a few nails. The furniture he made meant to remain long after his time to leave this world had come and gone, a part of his legacy reaching out into the world to hold others up for years to come. He was born into that vocation both physically and spiritually. Time with him was church, and I hung onto the words of every sermon he preached.

I can't count the number of times I've been saved by someone else. I'm can't even guarantee that I've thanked them all, but I can guarantee that during the weeks I spent there that summer, they both saved me. Minute by minute, I was brought closer to salvation and a truer sense of myself than I had ever felt before. By the time I was ready to go home, those last month's felt like just another nightmare I couldn't wake up from; I was awake now, revitalized, sitting at the table drinking my version of coffee and snatching the funnies every chance I could get. Each time making my grandmother laugh. See, I was invincible.

TWENTY-EIGHT

The Storm

It was my senior year, and I was more than ready for it to start and be over all at the same time. That last year of high school feeling like that last lap around the track to finish running the mile. You can see the finish line, but it feels so far away and your body burning like you've already been running for an eternity. Everything seems to take so much longer when you're young. It's when you get older, you're reminded of how precious each minute is, and they're all just flying down the tracks at a thousand miles an hour. You go from an hour sitting in class equating to a day to an hour reading a book gone in an instant. Time is a fickle mistress that controls us all, and we all bow to her omnipotence and beg for more at one time or another.

My summer away had healed the parts of me that needed it and being back had not flung me into the nightmare I had once been living in after that night. That's not to say I wasn't still running from the darkness at every turn on those days. I couldn't escape it with my eyes closed, but I had some reprieve during the day. I'd have the nightmare at least once a week, but that was a slow week for that van or those stairs. I was still able to get some sleep, unlike those before, where the darkness around me would terrorize me during those daylight hours as well. I could tell that Jess and Jo had managed to find their own distance from that night and were just as excited as I was to get this last year of school over and done.

I only took it as seriously as I needed in order to graduate. It might not have been the best choice, but it was the one I had made. Barely skating by in each class and rarely attending them as well. I'm not unintelligent by any means. I'm actually more intelligent than I usually give myself credit for. It just all seemed like a giant waste of time to me. My life was not going to be defined by whether I received a C or an A in English. I would still continue to exist, and my future wasn't going to be made or broken by my high school GPA. At least that's how I justified it. The truth is, I was still just a dumb kid making bad decisions thinking I knew everything when in actuality, I didn't know anything.

That's where I existed that year, locked between ignorance and invincibility. I knew I could accomplish anything; somehow, I pretended that meant I didn't have to do anything in the process. I was wrong. I could rattle off a hundred such instances that year, but I'm not sure that's the point of all this.

It was just another day, one I didn't want to have to deal with, and one I decided lunch with a friend at the mall sounded much more entertaining than whatever class it was I should have been in at that time. Oblivious to everything going on around me that day, other than the time and trying to decide what it was, I was hungry for and wanted to eat. We settled into those uncomfortable metal chairs and enjoyed a carefree lunch discussing whatever we could think of, except the weather. Not to be ignored, just as we were finishing, the bottom fell out, and it began to pour buckets. We couldn't see the first row of cars outside in the parking lot. It had turned on a dime out there, and nothing else existed past that giant glass wall.

I had to pick up my brother and sister in just a few minutes from that same junior high I started my life in this town attending. Something wasn't right. The color of everything on the other side of that glass turned an unnatural shade of green. It was one of those signs you knew to look for when the weather changed so quickly. The glass now looked as if it were breathing in and out, and I knew at any moment it could shatter into a million pieces. We stood frozen, in awe of nature barreling its way through and leaving what we knew was a path of destruction in its wake. Holding my breath as I waited for what I assumed was about to be the end of it all until the sky lightened and the rain slowed. I might have been able to run from the darkness in my dreams, but there's no way to escape nature if she's hungry enough to take you.

I exhaled for the first time in what felt like days. My lungs burning at the intrusion of the air bringing them back to life. The electricity still hovering close after the storm had cleared out. I looked over to my friend, who also looked to be tasting air again for the first time, and nervously laughed. Looking around the entire food court, we were the only two left standing there square in the middle. A sacrifice to our own lunacy had things gone differently. I gave her a hug and ran out the door to jump in my car and fly down the road to snatch up the siblings before anyone was the wiser that I hadn't been in class like I was supposed to be.

As I headed in that direction, the rain started in again like it had just moments before there at the mall. I couldn't see the road I was driving on and pushed forward blind at a snail's pace. I could have run into anything and never seen it until it was too late, but I kept going. I was maybe a mile from the school but felt as if I were already being lifted away to some munchkin-filled land. I couldn't guarantee that my tires were still on the road or that I was still driving in a straight line. For a moment, I thought, this is what it must feel like to be caught in the middle of the darkness. Unable to tell up from down, just surrounded by nothingness with no escape until it decided to release you. I was trapped in a prison of my own making. I should have pulled over and waited it out, but instead, I continued on, not knowing just how I was ever going to find my way.

I can't remember if I saw the turn or if I just somehow knew it was there. Muscle memory is a real thing when you've driven the same route repeatedly for over a year. All I know is I couldn't see anything. The rain looked as if it were coming from all directions at once, swirling around my car as the torrent of water pressed in harder. I managed to line myself up behind the cars waiting outside of the school and only hesitated for a moment before the crack of thunder shook the world around me like an earthquake. I couldn't stay here and wait to see if I was going to be sucked into some vortex and flung across the football field. So I took a deep breath, forwent the umbrella for fear of becoming an unwilling nanny without a bottomless carpetbag, and ran as quickly as possible into the school.

Walking inside, every child was sitting down the hallway, back against the wall with their heads between their knees and their arms covering the backs of them. This was the typical, kiss your ass goodbye position during a tornado, as if any of us truly believed that somehow being curled up against the wall staring at the floor was going to save us if the roof was ripped off and nature had her way. Refusing to sink down to the floor, I walked the length of the hallway in search of the back of the head of both my siblings. I wasn't having any luck and turned down one of the longer back hallways to make my way down to the bathroom at the very end of it. I made it just about halfway when all the lights went out, and I stood there in the darkness, the only light coming from the end of the hallway I'd just turned off from. The electricity hadn't failed, only this corridor seemed to be affected, the very end of it cloaked in complete blackness. I couldn't make out the bathroom doorway that I knew stood there waiting for me.

I stood frozen, waiting. My survival response always being to stand exactly where I am and not move. Surely whatever it was that might want to hurt me won't bother me at all if I just stand frozen. I believe this to be the least effective form of survival skills, but somehow, I've managed to escape each situation up until now. I was hoping my luck hadn't run out and that not fleeing in terror from the darkness was the right move at this moment. I could still see the light barely reaching down the hallway far behind me, and I couldn't help but think it would all disappear into the darkness in front of me, that it would all be swallowed up in an instant if only it chose to. As sure as I thought I was that I had walked directly into my nightmare, something wasn't right. It wasn't that ominous feel I would expect if I had been surrounded by such evil. My hair wasn't standing on end like it had there that night sitting on that picnic table. This was not the same. I waited there at the edge of darkness, the storm swirling outside, the thunder shaking the building off its foundation.

I had attended school here. I had seen the few ghosts that roamed the hallways, most attached to other kids or the faculty that worked here for years. As far as I could tell in the short amount of time I was here, there wasn't one specific to this place. There was no reason for me to be here like this, not one I knew of anyway. So, I waited. The thunder shook the building again, and the tornado sirens could barely be heard off in the distance over the battering rain, and still, I waited for what was holding me here. The lights flickered a few times, and I could see her near the end of the hallway when they did. I contemplated moving in her direction, but she wasn't ready for me yet. I wasn't the only one waiting. The unknown doesn't just grab hold of us and keep us locked in fear. We are all held petrified by it, whether we're dead or alive.

One more flicker, and she had moved closer now. I'd seen her, and she knew it. It was up to her to make the decision to acknowledge me or disappear into the darkness all over again. The thunderstorm outside only getting stronger, the air thick with the electricity from the ground lightning, and the wind howling in a way that only made me feel more anxious at the realization that we were smack dab in the middle of this storm. The walls creaking and the windows whistling, I started to wonder if I should be in that "kiss my ass goodbye" position or not. It felt more appropriate right then. The entire school was trembling as if it were going to be ripped from its foundation and pulled into another dimension, the sound of a freight train tearing its way down the hallways. Everyone else focused on that spot on the floor they all hoped if they stared at it and prayed just right, they'd come out of this untouched, other than the panic and trauma they'd carry around for the rest of their lives each time the clouds darkened off in the distance or the wind blew just the right way.

The sense of her getting closer yet reached out to me, and I knew she was ready. I stepped forward just as the lights flickered once more, and I found myself at an arm's length from her. She was flawless, absolutely beautiful. Her sash and crown in place, and her dress this puffy-sleeved purple atrocity from that decade. She radiated something I had never seen in a ghost before. She was confident in who she was, even if who she was didn't actually exist here any longer. I was suddenly aware of my water-soaked hair and clothes and the drops working their way down my arms and face. That's why I had been headed toward the bathroom to dry off, but now I stood in front of one of the homecoming court herself looking like a drowned rat.

She wasn't nearly as bothered by my appearance as I had suddenly become, and when she smiled at me, I forgot to care about it myself. Here I was, standing in front of the infamous ghost of the junior high that I thought for sure didn't really exist while a tornado ripped its way through the world outside. Maybe that's why it was now, no one else to pay attention to what was going on, to have me alone with no one the wiser as to her existence. The urban legends left to live on in perpetuity, and she deserved forever after what I assumed she'd been through that night. I smiled back at her with that thought and waited for her story, for her need to be heard to pour out of her just like the rain from the clouds was now. There was no story, no regrets other than her choice of a ride home. She had somehow managed to find her way past those moments left undone all on her own over the decades locked away here. There was only one thing she needed to say, only one thing holding her back from finally letting go.

"Thank you for seeing me. I've been waiting for someone to truly see me just once more. I think I needed to be sure I had actually existed in the first place and wasn't just the manifestation of a ghost story echoing these halls. I had lived, and I loved my life. It was a good night to go. Don't tell anyone I'm gone now. Wouldn't want them to think it's just a school or anything," and with a smile, she was gone.

I laughed so loud that I scared the kid closest to the hallway entrance at the far end that he squealed at the sound of it, which only made me laugh louder. I must have looked like a crazy person to the teachers who peered down to where I was, the storm outside still raging and me laughing like I'd just heard the best joke with no one else in sight. Shaking my head, I walked the rest of the way down to the bathroom to clean up, still chuckling with each step.

Ask anyone today, and she's still there. Still infamous. Still a warning to kids not to get into the car of someone you don't know, and yet still, she's gone.

TWENTY-NINE

Into the Dark

Dead.

A word I've grown used to hearing all my life. I've been surrounded by it in one way or another from almost as far back as I can remember. This time it meant something different. There was so much attached to that four-letter word that it took me a minute to process exactly what it meant. It was almost as if I'd forgotten all language, and the world was filled with just noise, and none of it making sense.

I'd seen the dead so often, I sometimes forget that they were once someone's friend or relative. You listen to them so often, you're lost in what they need to say, not that they used to be. I had never known anyone who died. Never been to a funeral for someone I was connected to or loved. I find it ironic now in a manner of speaking. Surrounded so much by those lost to have never lost anyone of my own. However, this one, I couldn't wrap my head around this one. I couldn't make it real because

I had pushed myself so far away from them that there were moments, I forgot they even existed.

The man that I had forgotten, yet couldn't forget, was dead. I couldn't concentrate enough to be concerned with the details as to how or when. The files in my mind that had been locked away flew open, and memories slid their way into every crevice, any spot they could find to hide with the sole purpose of jumping out to scare me when I was least expecting it. I felt like I was supposed to cry. That maybe I was even expected to cry, but there were no tears. I couldn't force myself to mourn someone I had never really known. Sure, he participated in giving me life, but he wasn't a witness as to who I had become or how I lived. A name on a piece of paper or attached to a branch on the family tree, that's all. Even though I didn't think of him included in that group when I used the word family, I guess the world still did. Society expected more from me at this moment than I was willing to give, and I refused to mar anyone's memory with fake emotion.

The funeral was arranged for that weekend, and I would be one of the few people in attendance. I anguished about it every day up until we left, trying to decide if I wanted to go or not. In the end, I think I needed to be sure it was really him and that he was really gone. I had spent so much time afraid that he'd show up out of the blue to claim my brother and me, taking us away from the life and happiness we had become accustomed to that I needed to see him there. I needed to be sure.

My mom, brother, and I loaded ourselves into the car for the drive to see the end of a nightmare as it was covered in earth and buried. I spent the hours in the car doing everything I could to reassess and categorize the rogue memories running around my brain like a schoolgirl running and giggling back and forth, trying to entice me into a game of tag. Although, I couldn't help the thoughts wandering off into the why of it over and over again. Of all people who should have had regrets and something to say, why had I not seen him? Why had he not come to find us to try and somehow make it better?

It was that thought that pushed me into the anger, into the rage. Maybe he didn't regret it or think that he had done anything wrong at all. How is that even possible? Each thought making me angrier. I deserved an apology. I had earned one long ago, and he had refused to even consider it or else, surely, he would have offered one up willingly. Did he have no remorse when it came to the things he had put us through? Again, how is that possible? It can't be. With that last thought, I was sure that I'd see him there standing next to his coffin wanting to clear his conscience in order to let go, and I wasn't sure I wanted to let him. Could I ignore him if he was there and leave him trapped that way? He had kept us trapped for what seemed like an eternity. Didn't he deserve the same caged feeling we had to live through?

It was a difficult decision to consider, and I guess it shouldn't have been. I mean, if I were a better person, of course, I'd want him to not be tethered here that way, right? No, it couldn't be a reflection on me, only the pain pushing its way through the cracks to try and control the decision with fear. Shaking it off, I tried to concentrate on something else, and I couldn't. There was no letting it go until the next day when we walked toward the gravesite for the service.

He wasn't there, and I couldn't tell you if I was more hurt or relieved at that moment. Honestly, it was a bit of both, and I felt my mother exhale next to me as we walked up to the casket. My brother cried, releasing the thought of a father he never knew and enjoying the few fun memories he had. He was blessed with having been so young when we escaped. Only the fun moments when we would visit were attached to this man for him. My mother and I sat and waited. We waited and watched as the last prayers were spoken, and they began to lower him into the ground. Holding our breath as we waited for the sound of the first few handfuls of dirt to hit the wood below, and that next breath somehow felt a little lighter. It was done. The one living nightmare I had been the most afraid of was dead and buried, and it was one ghost I was glad to be free from.

It was a few weeks later, the end of the school year, and my high school career just days away. The world was out there just for me, and I couldn't wait to find my way out into it and explore it all. In what had to be one of the last parties I remember attending, just hanging out with a few friends on the couch doing all the things we still weren't supposed to be doing and laughing about nothing. My life had become more mine than I had ever felt it was before. Now, I'm sure there are a lot of reasons for that, but the turning point in my world happened with just a handful of dirt.

My thoughts would find their way back there every once in a while, and I'd catch that memory that had been hiding and file it away properly. There wasn't the fear attached to them any longer, the unknown had been ripped from those fears, and the memories were just that, one of those faded pictures on a postcard. One nightmare had disappeared forever.

It was nice out that night, and we all found our way into the yard, laid out on blankets looking at the stars, and fluttered back and forth between talks of the future and one stupid topic after another. I don't know what it was, but in an instant, I knew I was no longer alone. I couldn't see anyone or anything, but I knew it was there. The hairs all over my body standing on end at its presence. I could feel it close. I could feel its familiar tug at my fears, its attempts to drown me in thoughts of the unknown, but I could see it now. I understood why it felt so familiar; it had been my constant companion my whole life. A darkness filled with fear, filled with the unknown, with pain and all the things you're scared of lurking in the shadows.

It wasn't unknown anymore, and there wasn't any fear remaining within me. It was time to face whatever it was looming in the darkness, whatever it was waiting for me in that van and on those stairs when I closed my eyes. I knew exactly who was there in the shadows waiting for me now-just another ghost waiting to be heard.

Now that he was dead and I knew he couldn't hurt me again, maybe now I might be ready to listen. Maybe, just maybe, he'd realize he'd have to use his words and not his hands for a change. As I stood up and looked over at my friends, my family, I smiled and took a little walk into the darkness.

INTO THE DARK

www.ingramcontent.com/pod-product-compliance
Lightning Source LLC
Chambersburg PA
CBHW031537310726
48971CB00008B/2517